I0610399

E.A. Maynard

BEARMAN

A Road of No Return

E.A. Maynard

Bearman: A Road of No Return
Copyright © 2020 by Gremlin Publishing
    All rights reserved. No part of this book may be
used or reproduced in any manner whatsoever without
written permission except in the case of brief quotations
embodied in critical articles or reviews.
    This book is a work of fiction. Names, characters,
businesses, organizations, places, events and incidents
either are the product of the author's imagination or are
used fictitiously for satirical purposes. Any resemblance
to actual persons, living or dead, events, or locales is
entirely coincidental.
        For information contact:
        E.A. Maynard
        info@eamaynard.com
        http://www.eamaynard.com
        Book and cover design by E. A. Maynard
        ISBN: 978-1-7343265-2-9

PREFACE

Bearman: A Road of No Return came to answer questions that was left unanswered in Country Secrets. The biggest question was how Scott Bearman became the way he was and what made him so powerful.

There were many other minor questions about inside jokes or comments that get answered from Country Secrets. These answers turned out to create the story and builds up the next book.

Finding these answers to these questions gave me a rush. This book started out to be a small novella, but the story took hold and wanted to be told. To make this a story that would be worth its purpose, I did not hold it back and let it go where it wanted.

Most of all, this book is meant for your entertainment. I hope you enjoy the story and where it leads you.

If you want to know about Country Secrets, you can go to www.eamaynard.com to learn more. You could also find all the books published by me.

CONTENTS

ACKNOWLEDGMENTS

Nothing is done without support and encouragement from those around me. I am thankful to my friends and family who have been there to encourage me to write.

Who I am most thankful is for those who read my books and like them enough to tell me how they enjoyed it.

CHAPTER ONE

I WAS A FULL MONTH into school and driving my beat-up 1979 brown Firebird. I had made it to my sophomore year of High School, and I had a good feeling it would be a good year. It might also be the joint that I was smoking as I drove down the country roads on my way in. You might ask who I am. My name is Bearman, at least that is what my friends call me. My full name is Scott Bearman and I am 16 years old. If you saw me, you would think I looked very average with my black hair, brown eyes, and a reddish tint to my dark suntan.

By the time I pulled into the school's parking lot, I saw my buddy Duke getting out of his car. He nodded at me and started to walk towards me. When he got to my car, I was getting out with my backpack and turned to look at him. He started to laugh when he saw my red eyes and said: "I know why you chose a cooking class to start your day." I think the class was called home economics and the teacher never let me do any of the cooking. I was lucky that the teacher understood that I needed an elective and she passed me with an B in that class. By the time I got out of the class each day, my high would have gone away and I had to deal with the rest of the day.

As I passed through the halls, I would stop and talk with my friends between classes. On this day, I was talking with a girl named Sara that I had been dating for a few months, and Duke. We were making plans and a guy who I kind of knew, stopped by us. He stood there looking at me. I stopped talking and asked this guy what he wanted, but I didn't think I was too nice about it.

He said, "Bearman, I heard that you always have some."

With nothing more said, I asked him what he was asking for. When he moved in closer to tell me what he wanted, I smelled the weed on him and knew what he wanted. He thought he was whispering, but his voice was loud enough for Sara and Duke to hear. They laughed at him while he said that he was looking for a pinner or a nice joint.

I could not help but smile when I asked him, "Who told you to talk to me?" He shrugged his shoulders and said that his friends know you. Instead of pushing it more, I wanted to get rid of the guy, so I pulled out a pinner and said that he could have it for five bucks. He handed me a five-dollar bill and ran off with it. That small pinner would only be good for a person, maybe two. I was not going to worry about what he would do with it.

Sara asked why I had that little joint in school. I explained that I was going to go out to the football field during gym class to smoke it. I would have to do without, but that is OK. I knew that I was going to meet up with a buddy in Fostoria and he seems to always have plenty of weed. I met this guy Mark through another friend, but we had become friends at that first meeting.

Now Sara, Duke and I had only a few moments before we had to get into English class. I hated that class and I thought Duke did too. It was not that we were bad at the subject, but the teacher treated the guys in her class poorly. Sara enjoyed screwing with Duke and me in that class. It seemed that the teacher really loved her. Sara with her black hair, brown eyes, and athletic body looking too hot to be with me. She was a sweet girl in front of everyone, but when she was out of view of most adults, Sara was a wild one.

I loved that she was as crazy as I was, but she knew how to hide it. From when I first met Sara at a party, we clicked. At that time, it seemed that Sara, Duke, and I were almost always found with each other. I think that we were so close because we were able to be ourselves around each other. Sara and I also had biological fathers who liked to blame us for any problems in their lives. I don't think Sara's dad ever put a hand on her, but I could not say the same thing. I tried to hide my abuse from everyone until one day that Duke saw it happening and tried to help me. That was not a good day, but luckily when I became old enough, I could choose not to go see him, and I don't think he minded. In fact, I think that made him happy.

After we got through the English class, we talked in the hall. Since we had no more classes together for the rest of the day, we discussed what we had going on. Sara asked what Duke and I were doing after school. Before we got to answer, she told us that she was going to meet her friend Jenny. It did not dawn on me why Sara looked at Duke and smiled when she said that. Sara's smile went away when I said that I had to work till seven and go meet up with another friend. Duke jokingly said "You have other friends? I thought we were the only ones that can put up with you."

With a kiss-off look on my face, Sara jumped in and asked Duke if he wanted to hang out with her and Jenny. If I remember properly, he wanted to, but he told Sara that he would be watching his little sister, which did not make her happy either. Before she had a chance to say anything more, the bell rang. We all went our different ways to get to the next class. Sara was only a few doors down from her next class, but Duke had to run to the gym that was in the middle of the building. As for me, I had my next class at the end of the building in a farm class. That teacher hated me too, but that was because I went out of my way to screw with him. I would be late to that class on a regular basis. When I passed the principal's office, I would stop and talk with someone. I talked about something random and they would give me a pass for being late to class. I had to believe that they considered it a way to save them time. That teacher liked to send me to see the principal for any reason to get me out of his class.

The rest of the day was event-less, and I went to work at the scrap yard. It was not the type of job you did when you cared about your lungs. My job was to get the copper out of motors after they have gone through a burning process. I would grab a mostly cooled small motor and use my tools to get the copper out of the motors. Most times the motors were small enough I could have picked up with my own hands. But that day, I got the big motor that was as tall as me. I remember that I had to use the big and heavy tools to get the copper out. By the time I got the first motor done, I was exhausted. I stepped out the doors to the outside and had a cigarette. As I was taking my first hit, my boss came to me and told me that he was going to smoke a joint. I knew well enough that meant he was saying that we were going to smoke a joint.

That made it a little nicer and my muscles felt much better. Then he grabbed the forklift and pulled the motor out of my bay. He placed a four –by– four– by– four bin full of small motors for me to work on in its place. I worked for another two hours when my boss came back and told me it was time to go. He had already taken his shower and I was always the last to use the mudroom's shower. As the low man on the totem pole, I was happy if I got a lukewarm shower. I got in a habit to be very quick in my showers and got out as soon as the water stopped looking black.

Since my workday was done, I drove to meet up with my friend Mark, in Fostoria. I met this guy at a party a few months back. We would hang out now and again. I never knew how knowing Mark would change my life. At that time, we were only two high school guys who liked to get high and make bad jokes that we found funny. Mark's place was a nice blue house that needed to have a paint job. I remember walking up the sidewalk wondering why they did not take care of their place. The other houses around him were well taken care of. Mark also hated when I went into his house, which told me he didn't like the way his home looked.

When I showed up, Mark introduced me to his cousin who had moved in. His cousin looked like he had not been clearheaded for quite some time. His mom was in the kitchen drinking, but she had a hard life from what I heard. Her husband and Mark's father died in a car accident a few years back. Mark told me that after the accident, the life insurance paid off the house and had a little money left over. His mom kept getting worse about her drinking as time went on. That day, you could see how she was skinnier than most people with her body frame. Mark's little brother basically was being raised by Mark and his Grandma. Seeing Mark's family, it surprised me how happy Mark seemed.

I was not at Mark's place for long when Mark said that we had to go see his guy. I figured he was out of weed. We drove down Union Street until we showed up to a house by an old pizza shop. We walked up the stairs where a big black guy with two Dobermans barking at us sat on his porch. I assumed that it was his house. While I stood on the top step, Mark and this guy went into the house. It was not long when they came back out and he left the dogs inside. The guy known as Deatz, looked at me, then said, "I take it this is your first. Well, you need to relax or you're going to make someone nervous. Remember that nervous people do stupid things." I simply said OK since I did not know what he was talking about.

Mark knew what was happening. He told me that we needed to get going and we took off. This time, we drove to Kmart's parking lot and sat in the car when another guy soon pulled up. Mark pulled out a large bag of weed and a bag of cocaine. That is when I realized that Deatz meant that it was my first-time selling drugs. He was right and Mark knew that too, if you don't count selling a joint every once and while.

Mark started to get out of the car and told me to get out and stand there like I was pissed. All I could think is it was like something from a TV show. The difference from a TV show was that the dealers were normally adults or college kids selling to kids like us. This was the other way around. I remember seeing a Bowling Green State University parking pass on his car. While I was looking around to make sure there were no cops, I noticed this blond-haired pale guy. He handed Mark a white envelope, which I assumed was money. Mark, in turn, gave the guy the drugs. I fought my urge to tell the guy to get some sun but making jokes would not have helped.

For some reason, I got an adrenaline rush from doing that deal. It also got me going more when Mark reached in the envelope and gave me fifty dollars. When I asked him why he was giving me the money, he told me that we were partners now and he would not screw his partner. We stopped back at Deatz's place and this time I stayed in the car. Mark went up with the money to Deatz's door. When the door opened, Mark walked in, then the old heavy wood door shut behind him. I figured they were counting the money and talking. The reason I figured they were talking was Deatz came out with Mark and leaned into the open window. Deatz then dropped a quart bag in my lap and said, "This is my welcome gift. I always take care of my guys. Mark also speaks highly about you. Let's see if he is right." He did not wait for me to answer when he walked away, and Mark got in. We were back off to his place

Walking into Mark's house, we talked about the deal along with other deals that he had set up. I saw his mom laying on the couch as we walked to the stairs. "Mark, should I watch what I say around your family?" Mark replied to my question with shaking his head to say no while making a face. He was already walking up the stairs and I followed him up to his room. When I walked into his room, Mark was holding his rolling papers and was saying "Oh crap, Oh Crap, I can't believe this." I had no idea why he was freaking out. He ran downstairs and I heard him yelling at his mom. It sounded like Mark was asking how she was going to pay for the drugs she took from him.

All I could think was holy crap. I could not imagine having that kind of life. From how his mom looked when we came in, she must have gotten into his stash. When Mark got back up, he confirmed what I thought. He went on about how his mom, three of her friends and a cousin came over, and took what they found in his room. Mark looked scared as he got into a box that he had under his dresser.

I asked him "What is going on? I know it sucks that your mom took your pills." Mark started to shake his head and I figured he was going to cry if I was not there. He told me that the pills where valued at two grand and he did not have the money to pay Deatz back. From the little bit I got to see of Deatz, he was not someone who would be free with his money. So, I could understand why he was scared.

"Bearman, I know Deatz has a scarier boss and Deatz tries to do what he needs to, so his boss does not see weakness." Mark took a deep breath and continued speaking. "I am going to die because my mom can't get past my dad's death. If I die, she will certainly end up killing herself with an overdose. Who knows what will happen to Jay"?

There was no question that Mark was freaking out, so I told him that I might be able to help. Mark counted out the money in the box he pulled from his dresser. He told me he had five hundred dollars. I told him that I had a ton of Ritalin. I followed with how I sell them for five dollars a pill and have more coming. The only question I had for him was how much time we had till Deatz would ask for his money.

Mark walked back and forth and said that he could push it off for a week, but after that, he would not let it slide. Now it was up to us to plan how to move my pills. The problem I was seeing was Mark only pushed weed, speed, cocaine, and some downers. It took him a little time to understand that we would be pushing to the smart kids. Those kids who have always been at the top of the class.

As he thought about it, I rolled a joint with my weed and lit it up. After a big hit and a deep inhale, I coughed and felt very relaxed. "Wholly crap, this is some good shit. So, let me say this, I have over three hundred pills I was saving for midterms. If we sell them at twenty dollars for four and make it a minimum, we would only need to get about thirty-eight deals each. I know about ten kids that would put out sixty dollars or more for their supply. There are a few others that would buy some, so I can reach my half in time. Do you have anyone to go to?" Mark exhaled when I finished talking. He only said he thinks so.

What kind of answer was that, was all I could think about. This was the first time I got pissed while smoking weed. Normally I would be giggling and asking for pizza rolls. Instead, I was trying to help someone who did not make any effort. I hoped that I did not regret doing this. I would be tied to him if people found out and then Deatz might come to me for the money if Mark didn't pay. I took the joint from Mark and smoked more while he only sat there. Then it hit me, and I could not focus. I leaned back and zoned out.

An hour or so had passed and Mark decided that we needed to run to Taco Bell. He believed that he had to have some tacos, or he would die. I was right there with him thinking the same way. We rushed out the door and were off down the road. I was sobering up a bit while I drove my old beater. It might have been a crappy car, but for my first car, I loved it. My friends would joke to me about it being a death trap. I was a little embarrassed but working at a scrap yard part-time did not make me a lot of money.

I could see Mark sobering up too, so I asked him if he could actually sell the pills or do, we need to come up with another plan. He sat quietly for a minute and said that he could. I did not feel reassured, but I had nothing else to say to help. I liked Mark and I did not want my new friend to have anything happen to him. He put in a tape that I had labeled "HIGH". It was a collection of weird songs that were fun to listen to while I was high. One of the Doors songs came on and made me laugh. I guess I was not completely sober.

After we got our tacos, we went and sat in the parking lot across the street. Mark started to shovel tacos in his mouth before I was parked. I grabbed the bag, turned off my car, and went to sit on my hood. Mark came out for the food and possibly to talk with me. We ate those tacos like we had not eaten in days. In minutes the only proof that we had tacos were the bag and wrappers.

CHAPTER TWO

WEDNESDAY CAME AROUND and I was happy that I had made just over a thousand. I forgot how many of my classmates where focused on their grades. I even had one guy buy two hundred dollars at one time. No one spent less than sixty dollars at a time. I could only think that Mark, who going to a larger school must have been doing better than I was. The rest of the day I attended classes, flirted with Sara, and made deals with some other kids. The kids were looking for something extra. Most of my sales were a dime bag of weed, but I was trying to expand with Mark's connection to Deatz. When the school day was done, I walked out to my car.

Sara stood next to my driver's side door while I walked up towards her. I was only two cars away when she yelled at me. "You owe me a dinner, hurry your ass up." I did not remember that we made plans, but it would not be the first time she decided we had a date without talking to me. Taking her out was better than anything else I had planned. Plus, she knew that I did not have to work in the scrapyard, so I had no excuse as far as she was concerned.

We drove to Findlay because Sara wanted to eat at a restaurant called Friendly's. They had good sandwiches, but Sara wanted to go so we could share a vanilla hot fudge sundae. She loved the big glass it came in and I had to order it for myself so she could say that she was helping me with it. She always said,

"Are you getting yourself a hot fudge sundae?" I did not mind since I loved ice cream. I don't remember what we talked about, but we laughed and held hands. It was a good time until we were walking back to my car.

I did not realize that some guy who I pissed off were there waiting for me. Sara had gotten into my car and I was walking back to the driver's side. That is until someone pushed me into the back of my car. As I went to turn around, there was a fist punched into my upper back. What a dumb ass was all I could think. You don't punch someone in the back of the shoulder, which does nothing unless they are already hurt. I had taken enough punches to know two things. The first thing was how to take a hit, the other is where to punch to cause the most pain. The first thing was because I had been punched enough in the past by my father Cameron.

I did not wait for whoever was trying to beat me up to figure out what to do. I spun around and kneed the guy in the bladder. He fell to the ground and peed himself when his buddy came to help his friend. Dumb asses must travel in groups because the guy was yelling as he came my way. When he got close enough, I dropped down to become a ball. He did not have time to stop as he ran into me and fell onto his buddy's chest. I heard them both make a noise of pain and that made me happy.

Now there was time to see who it was. I never knew the guy's name as he was someone who I embarrassed at a party. He was trying to flirt with Sara, but she was not having anything to do with him. He was not taking the hint, so Sara gave me the sign she does when she needs some help. When I got there, he was becoming rude and he started to reach out to grab Sara. I was not going to let some creep touch her. With his arm outreached, I grabbed it and pushed him to the wall. While he was against the wall, I explained that a lady should not be treated in the manner he was. He tried to say something, but it was not nice, and I added some pressure to his arm. I was not going to break his arm, but I did want him to know not to be rude.

I gave him an option to receive more pain or he could leave after telling Sara that he was sorry. He apologized and I let him go. Once I took my hands off him, he fell on a table full of drinks. Everyone started to laugh at him, as he was covered in beer and some food. When I turned around to go to Sara, I saw Mark for the first time standing next to Duke. They had their hands on another guy's shoulders.

That was the night Mark became our friend. Mark and Duke explained that the guy they held was about to go after me while I dealt with his friend. The rest of the party was quiet and we hung out talking. Duke, Mark, Sara, and I talked about pointless things. We found a mostly empty room and smoked a joint and I did not think anymore about the guy being rude to Sara.

That is until he attacked me outside of Friendly's. It was time for him and his buddy to learn a lesson. My step-dad made sure I had a crowbar in my car at all times. His reason was that my driver's side door was welded shut. If I needed to break a window or pry something, it would be very helpful. I found another reason to keep it by my seat. I reached into my car and pulled out the black crowbar. Sara sounded concerned and kept saying we need to go before they get up.

I did not plan to let them get up too quickly. When I got back to them, the friend was getting up. That was till I hit him right above his knee. He dropped and I dragged him out of the way of my car. The first guy laid on the ground crying, covered in his own piss. I hit him once in his arm with the crowbar. I swung that crowbar like I was teeing off at a golf course. I gave them both a warning not to ever come after my girl or me, adding that they would be smart to turn around and leave if they ever see us. Neither of them answered me, but I didn't think either of them would try anything again.

Sara and I got down the road when she asked who they were and why they came after me. It did not take much to remind her about what the guy did at the party. All I had to do was say that he was the guy from the party where we met Mark. I could see on her face the moment she remembered. Sara looked ticked and said that she was happy that I kicked his ass again. Never had I ever seen Sara so happy to see me fight.

We were not far from Fostoria going down route twelve when Sara asked if we could make a trip to Mosier Lake. Knowing what she was saying, there was no way I would have told her no. We came up to the golf course and I turned right onto Independence Avenue. It was only two miles till we got to the pull-off for Mosier Lake. As we pulled down the drive along the side of the lake, we played with each other's hands, arms, and legs. Once we got to a little opening about midway back, we got into the back seat as fast as we could.

After less than half an hour together, Sara started joking. She joked about how uncomfortable my old beat-up car was. She knew it was all I could afford, but it was better than nothing. We got ourselves together and back on the road before someone came to check why we were back there.

By the time we got into Fostoria, Sara said that she did not mean to make fun of my car. She reminded me that people have nicknamed it the death trap. I could not help but laugh. Friends have made jokes about how scared they were to be in my car.

I was not mad about her comment. Sometimes she worried about hurting my feelings or upsetting me. Part of that came with having a parent verbally beating you down. I held her hand and told her that I have thicker skin than to be hurt by that.

We got back to having a pleasant drive all the way back to her house. Sara made me feel better than any time I smoked weed or got drunk. That is why after I dropped her off, the rest of the drive back to my mom's house had passed before I realized it.

Walking in the house, my mom told me that I missed a call from Mark. It must have been close to nine at night, so I was not sure if Mark would still be up. It only took two rings when the phone was answered. It was Mark's younger brother Jay who answered the phone. He was a little shit who should be smacked a bit to knock some sense into him. After I told Jay who I was, he yelled Mark's name. It did not take long before Mark got on the phone.

"Bearman, I have to meet with Deatz tomorrow. Do you have your share of the money?" Mark sounded as he was still nervous while asking me about the money. I explained that I did better than expected and we could meet after school and go see Deatz. I figured that would be fine, but Marks told me that Deatz wanted to see him around noon. This was not the best timing as I had an exam that I could not miss.

I told Mark that I would skip out of school around my lunch. Then we could go together to Deatz around twelve-thirty or one. Mark and I did not talk much after that, as he only had one thing on his mind and was not interested in any other discussions.

I hung up and went to bed. I had not slept well, wondering what Deatz would do, kept me up. I did not know Deatz at all or how he would take it that I showed up for a meeting with Mark.

The next day, I went to school, but it was a blur. I remember talking to Duke and Sara as we did every morning. Once I said that I was skipping out once lunch comes, Sara wanted to join me. I felt bad when I had to tell her that I could not have her come with me, so she used it to her benefit. Sara had me promise that we would go bowling and bring her friend from

Gibsonburg.

I took my exam and went to a few classes, but I did not take anything in. I went through the motions until lunch. I ran out of the school and to my car. If someone was watching me, I did not even care. Mark was waiting for me, which means Deatz was waiting. Deatz did not come across as someone you keep waiting. So, I flew down the country roads as fast as I could.

Before I knew it, I was pulling in front of Mark's house. I was halfway out of the car when he came running out of his house. He jumped in the passenger seat while I climbed back into my seat. I did not wait for any small talk and got on the road. Without a word between us for two blocks, Mark broke the silence by asking me how much money I had on me. I was happy when I said that I got a thousand because two kids traded a month's worth of pills each on Monday. I sold all my pills.

Mark looked down at his feet and said he only got two hundred dollars from the pills I gave him. I didn't know how that was possible, so I asked how much money he had on him. While he is still looking down, he reached into a backpack that he had with him and pulled out some cash. By the time we pulled in front of Deatz's house, Mark said he had seven–fifty. This all made no sense to me, but we had to figure out something quickly.

Deatz must have seen us pull up because he walked out to his porch and waved us to come into his house. Mark waved back to him and I knew we were out of time. We walked towards Deatz, who was standing in the doorway.

Mark walked as if he were a child about to be scolded for doing something wrong. I did not want to show that I was scared. I had my head up and walked as if I had a purpose. I let Mark go up the stairs first into the door because he was already known.

When I got past the threshold, Deatz told me to shut the door and lock it. I shut it, but I did not lock it. If something went down that I had to run, I was not going to make it harder for myself. Deatz noticed it since he watched me but did not say anything. Mark sat down on a fake leather couch and I stood to the side of it. Deatz looked at me and then the door before asking why I was there. He was not happy, and I don't know if it had anything to do with me being there. I started to answer him until Deatz told me to shut up and told Mark to give him the money he owed him.

Mark pulled out the cash in his bag and put it on the coffee table in front of him. I followed suit and put a brown bag with my cash next to the cash Mark put down. Deatz looked at me again and told me to sit down, I did not argue, and I sat in a Lazy-boy chair. Once I did, Deatz's dogs came out from around it and jumped on my lap. At first, I figured I was about to become a dog chew toy. Then I was covered with slobber and dogs pushing for attention.

Deatz got up and took the dogs away, I told him I was ok with them. He sat back down and asked me again what I was doing there. Mark still had not said a word since we walked in and I did not figure he would. I realized then that Mark would not be able to help me do what I figured that Mark and I could do together. I was on my own to get things going. That is when I told Deatz that I came to make more money for all of us.

Deatz leaned forward and said "Who do you think you are? I'd been doing this since I was your age. I did not worry about school and made my money. Why shouldn't I whoop your ass right now?"

This was not the start that I hoped for, but it was a start. I quickly replied with "Let me put it this way. I have some guys that keep asking for me to supply them more than a dime or quarter at a time. I have a guy wanting some crystal and cocaine for a party he was going to. He will bring a grand tomorrow and I am expecting to get something from you. You see my car out there? It's a piece of shit and I am embarrassed every time my girl gets into it. I am not making enough working at a scrapyard, so I sell weed and other things I get from people. I believe I can move more drugs in the farm towns, as long as I have the supply."

I took it as a good sign when Deatz smiled. Then he pulled the cash on the table close to him. While he was putting the money in order to and counted it, he asked Mark if everything was there. Before Mark answered, I spoke up again. I told Deatz that Mark and I discussed partnering up to make more money as a team. He did not look amused with me jumping in till I told him that we still owed him two hundred dollars. The smile was gone now, and I kept talking. Before we left, I made him an offer to give me eight ounces of weed, cocaine, and crystal meth to see a nice return. I also had to promise that I would give him four hundred out of my profit to cover the delay.

Now I did not just take another step into the drug world but I jumped in with both feet. I had two weeks to bring back seven-hundred for the cocaine and meth, then eight hundred for the weed. This meant that I owed nineteen hundred. I would only be making over three hundred on the deal, but it was the only way to get in. By the time Deatz agreed to everything, he got me what I asked for and told Mark that he had a drop to make the following day. Mark spoke for the first time since we walked in with telling Deatz that he would not be late. With that, we were back out the door and in my car.

I drove us to the deli to get lunch. On the way, I asked Mark if he even sold anything or were all his deals lined up by Deatz. That is when he came clean and said that he was trying to sell but was not doing too good. Mark told me how scared he was of Deatz or he would just stop it all. It was ironic that I was pushing us more into it and Mark wanted out. He also told me that he needs the money to help pay the bills.

I thought about what Mark said for a moment. Then I said "You know, we need to build you up so you're not Deatz's delivery boy. I have a plan that won't need you to sell. I need to see if these guys who keep asking me to supply them are interested in what I have in mind. If I can get things set up, I can hopefully put us in a good place." With that said, I climbed out of my car and went into the deli to eat. I was hungry.

E.A. Maynard

CHAPTER THREE

THERE WERE NO WORDS for how excited I was. On Friday, I found the guy who wanted the crystal meth and cocaine. Once I told him that I had what he wanted, we walked back to the boy's locker room. Sitting on a bench, I showed the guy the product that I had in my backpack. He seemed happy and reached into his backpack. While his hand was in his bag, he asked what would happen if he took the drugs without paying.

I don't know if he was trying to be funny or if he was planning something, but I was not going to take a chance. I asked him if he ever saw a deer field–dressed. He had not, so I explained how it was not a difficult process, but it is messy. He looked confused till I explained that would be what I would do to him and if I didn't, my supplier would do worse. With that said, his smile went away, and he moved his hand around in his bag and pulled out some cash. As he was counting out, I told him that the price was twelve hundred. He tried to tell me how he would only pay a grand till I said I would go to another guy in the school I knew was big into his meth.

Luckily, I knew a handful of people who he was planning to sell to. It would have taken me longer to sell everything, but I knew I could do it and make more money. That is not what I wanted though. He agreed to the new price and we made the exchange. As he started to leave, I asked him if he wanted to make this a regular thing. He told me that he did, and he became the first guy in my plan to develop a network of smaller dealers. With twelve hundred, and another guy lined up who wanted a good amount of weed, I figured it would be a good day.

I went through school as I normally do. I went to my classes and made plans with Sara. She wanted to go see a movie after I got out of the scrapyard, but I had to meet up with a guy named Mick. This guy wanted to buy two ounces and that would have me more than halfway through my supplies. I also knew that this Mick guy was popular in his school. This could be a good connection and I did not want to lose it.

Sara and I made our plans for the weekend. She wanted to meet up at her friend's place in Gibsonburg. With that set up, Sara wrote down her friend's number and ran off. The only good thing about Sara walking away was that I got to see her cute little body move in a sexy little way. It seemed as though she did it for only me to see. Once she was out of sight, I went to my final class and finished my day. Then I was off to my real job. It was a reason for people not to ask where I got my money, plus I worked at the scrapyard before adding the extra income from selling.

It was always fun on my drive to work. I needed to change as I drove so I could start work and meet my quota. By the first stop sign, I had already ripped off my shirt and had my work shirt in my hand. Once I got through Risingsun, I had already changed my shirt, my shoes were tossed in the back, and my pants were half off. Changing my pants was always the trickiest while I was going about sixty-five. If you want to get a sense of fear, bump the steering wheel with cruise control on while pulling on a pair of pants. Normally, by the time I got to work, I only had to tie my boots and grab a paper air mask.

It was an easy day at work, and I had another joint with my boss. I always asked him if doing what we did was normal to do on the job. He laughed every time I would ask because he knew I was hoping that he would change his answer and say yes, it is.

That never happened and he always told me that the real world is much harder. It seemed that day someone was helping me. I got my quota met an hour early and was lucky to get a shower with hot water. Typically, I was the last done and the last to use the shop shower. Since everyone there were big hulking guys compared to me, they had no issues emptying the hot water tank.

All cleaned up and ahead of schedule, I got moving. It was a short drive to get to Fremont from where I was. I was hoping that this Mick guy would be home. Mick was a friend of a guy I sold some joints to. The guy buying the joints told me about Mick and gave me his phone number. It took a few calls back and forth to catch each other, but when we did, we made a deal. We decided to meet up at a Kmart on Oak Harbor Road. For some reason, Kmart's parking lot had become a Friday night hangout. When I pulled in, I saw a group of kids off to the side away from all the cars, and another group toward the middle of the lot. When I was noticed by them, I parked between the groups, but a bit farther away from the store. I was on the edge of the parking lot light, but my car could be seen.

It must have been twenty minutes I sat there before this red Hair, pale kid with freckles came up to my car. When he got up to me, he said it would have been smarter to have parked with the customer cars. "Mick, I take it. Hop in the passenger seat and let's talk." He was already walking around when I finished talking. He walked as though he was sure of himself and looked like he could take a punch. That gave me some hope that this guy was not just starting to deal.

Mick sat down and looked around my car. The first thing he said was "how slow is your business?" It didn't bother me that he said it. I explained to him that my source could handle larger supply request,. Mick asked how much weed I had on hand, and if he wanted anything else, could I get it. This was our first time dealing with each other. Maybe he was trying to see how serious I was about this too.

I smiled and said "I currently have eight ounces on me. If you want something different, I don't carry anything on me. I could get the common stuff, but I need a heads up of how much and what is wanted. Then I will get it."

With that Mick pulled cash from his pocket and counted it out. He held out a stack and asked how much could he get for six hundred. I did the numbers in my head the best I could and offered him four ounces and a quarter bag.

Mick agreed and we made our exchange. Mick requested another four ounces of weed, fifty hits of Ecstasy, and two sheets of acid. I did not see any issues getting this and let him know what the cost of all that would be. With the conversation finished, Mick was off. I moved my car up to the front door of Kmart. Parking in the fire lane, I dug for some change and found a few dimes and two quarters. That was all I needed to make a call.

With my change in hand, I ran to a payphone and called Sara. There were two rings when a girl answered the phone. I did not know the voice, but I assumed it was Jenny. I said hello and before I said anything else, the girl got happy and said "Is this Scott, when will you be here? I've heard so much about you and Sara said you are coming here." When she took a breath, I told her that I would be on my way, but I still needed to know where she lived. She gave me the address and handed the phone to Sara. When Sara got on the phone, she started to tell me how she wanted to go see a movie called Powder. I did not know anything about it, so I told her that we could watch whatever she wanted.

It did not take me long to get to where Sara was. I parked in front of a white house with a large porch covering the front and part of the side.

As I put the car in park, Sara came out and sat on my hood.

When I got out of the car, she was acting like she was the girl in a Guns–n–Roses or Aerosmith video. It made me laugh and my hood was strong, so I was not worried about her being up there. She was swinging her hair around and giggling. I got to the front of my car and grabbed her feet, then pulled her to me getting myself a very nice kiss and a big hug. Sara asked what took me so long and I explained that I was doing some extra work to get a better car. She smiled and asked if we could test the back seat before I buy something. That, of course, put a big smile on my face.

While we were flirting and joking with each other, her friend came out and hugged Sara and me at the same time. When she let go of us, she told me that her name is Jenny. She was five feet and seven inches tall. If I had to guess, Jenny with her long light brown hair and brown eyes only weighed a hundred and ten pounds at best. She smiled and I noticed a little black mark between her nose and her right eye.

While I was looking at her, I asked Sara "Is this the girl you want Duke to meet?" Sara smiled and told me that was going to be a surprise. Then she told me that Duke was on his way to join us. I think Jenny realized what was going on and started to blush. Jenny started to ask me about Adam Byrd. I explained to her why we called him Duke and a few things about him as he pulled up.

It seemed funny to me that when Duke saw a girl, he was instantly attracted to her. The first thing he always did was put his hand on the back of his head as if he was rubbing it. I have no idea why he does that and when I asked him, he did not realize he was doing it. At least that was what he told me. Next, he had a few nervous movements he would do, but this time he did not get a chance.

Sara ran up, grabbed both of their hands, and pulled them up on the porch to the swing. As they stood in front of the swing, Sara went inside to grab the cordless phone. Duke grabbed the arm of the swing and asked Jenny if she would like to sit. Watching them, I wondered if Sara and I were that awkward at first.

Moments later she came running back out. She started repeating what movies were playing and what time. I knew she was calling the theater in Bowling Green since that was her first choice for theaters. That allowed me to at least say no to the movies we would not make it to based on show times. The three of them discussed the movies as I watched. Sara knew I would watch whatever she wanted to see. I did wonder what happened that she wanted to go watch Powder.

We never did make it to see a movie that evening. One conversation about the movies led to another topic and then to another. It was about ten o'clock when I said that I was going home. Duke said he was going too and as he got up, I noticed that he and Jenny were holding hands. What a sweet pair was my first thought. My next thought came when Sara jumped up on me wrapping her legs around my waist said, "Take me away as far as we can go."

Jenny and Duke laughed as I carried Sara to my car and sat her on my hood. I asked her where she wanted to go, then started to list off places far away. It seemed unlikely that some country kids would go to those places. She stopped and said that we would go to China or India and get lost in areas no one had explored. I agreed and told her that we should, and as normal, she said the line that we always said to each other. "We will go tomorrow or the next day or the day after that. We will go, just the two of us." It was fun to joke about it and also sad in a way. I knew we would never go to any of the places we listed off. We knew lots of older people who never even left the state of Ohio.

I gave Sara a passionate kiss because I was sixteen and that is what we did every chance we got. When we finished and I was climbing into my car, I looked over to see Duke and Jenny talking and being cute. Sara already told me she was staying at Jenny's, so I went straight home. Before I drove away, Duke knocked on my window and said he would be staying at my place. I gave him a thumbs up and got going. He was not far behind me as I saw him driving up behind me two miles out of Gibsonburg.

Two hours after we got to my place, we sat on the front porch smoking and talking. Duke wanted to talk about Jenny and find out what I thought about her. Around midnight though, we both were exhausted and called it a night.

The next day, I got up and was out the door around ten in the morning. I went out to meet up with two other guys I knew, and I wanted to see how Mark was doing. First I went to Findlay where I tracked down my first guy around noon. He made my life easier by buying two ounces and asked if I could supply him the same amount every week. Of course, I told him I could and we exchanged phone numbers to save time. I did not want to run around again if I knew where he would be to start with.

My next stop was Upper Sandusky. Considering it was south of Sandusky, Ohio, I always tried to figure out why it was called Upper Sandusky. I mostly thought about it to kill time while I drove. When I got into Upper Sandusky, I saw some kids my age walking and I asked them if they knew where I could find this last guy. Luckily, they knew him and said he was normally at Harris Smith Park on nice days. It made my day when I found him there sitting in the bed of his pickup truck.

Not seeing anyone else around, I pulled up next to him and asked if he was still looking to buy in bulk. He had to sit up and look at me for a moment before he remembered me. He got out of his bed and I got out of my car. It took about five minutes of small talk before he would discuss any deal. When we discussed making a deal, he bought my last two ounces and asked how soon I could get more for him.

Come to find out, this guy had a good thing going. He would sell his supply of weed within two or three days and could do more if he had it. From what he said, he normally got an ounce from a guy who would come up from Columbus every week. So, I told him that I would supply him as much as he wanted if he only bought from me. He agreed to that deal and we exchanged numbers.

Now I was off to see if Mark was home. I wanted to have him with me when I gave Deatz his money a week early and put a request in for more. I figure Deatz was not expecting me to even sell what I had, let alone come back early with a larger order. This ran through my head as I drove down the road. I could not help to play out the different conversations that might occur. I was excited as I knew I could get a new car in a few months if I kept this up.

Once I pulled up to Mark's house, I didn't see his car. I hoped that I would be lucky and he would be in there. The door opened before I got a chance to knock. A thirteen-year-old boy answered the door. It was Mark's younger brother Jay. He was a skinny kid who looked like he needed to be smacked across the face. When I asked Jay where his brother was, Jay increased my urge to smack him when he replied to me. He had a stupid look on his face when he asked what it was to me where his brother was. I took a step closer, looked down on this kid, and said "It matters to you. If you don't tell me where your brother is, I will backhand you till you learn some manners." He quickly said Deatz's name and shut the door.

Mark was at Deatz, which might be good for me. I got over there as fast as I could. I wanted to keep my word to Mark and get him out from under Deatz. I liked Mark and with what I had planned, I would need someone I could trust. Deatz had his front door open and the dogs sat on the porch.

I yelled into the house from the bottom of the steps. I was not going to take the chance that the dogs would remember me. There never has been a time that I wanted to get bitten by a dog. The dogs moved and were sitting at the top step with the rope tying them to the house became tight. I took the chance and stepped up two steps leaving a foot between the dogs and me.

When I went to yell again, I felt a cold wet dog's nose pushing on my hand. The first thought was oh crap, then I was relieved when I realized I was not being bitten. Now that I knew these dogs were more show, I walked up on the porch and knocked on the door frame. The dogs might not hurt me, but Deatz most likely kept loaded guns. I was not going to test his flexibility.

It was not long after my knocking that he came to the door. "What do you want?" Deatz was not in a happy mood when he said that, or he just stopped liking me, so I was hoping he was having a bad day. I responded by explaining how I was out already. That seemed to make him a little happier and got me invited in. As I followed him into his kitchen, I saw Mark sitting at the table. Mark was breaking down bundles of weed into smaller portions.

Deatz looked at me and asked if I was going to help. If I understood how dangerous Deatz was, I would have not told him to kiss my ass and be a lot nicer. I noticed that he reached for a gun in the back waist of his pants. I decided it would be best to get to the point and maybe the large request would make up for what I said.

"I need a pound of weed, two sheets of acid with a hundred tabs each, and fifty hits of ecstasy before Friday. I would also like an ounce to go today." I was right as I finished saying that, as he pulled his hand away from the gun and started to nod. With everything back to being an easy-going environment, I pulled out the money I had and counted it out.

When I handed him the cash, he gave me two hundred back telling me Mark was working that off as we spoke. Looking over at Mark, I asked how much was left till he was done. I did not wait for an answer and sat down at the table. I never had so many drugs in front of me at one time. My eyes must have been huge as I took my first real look at what all was on the table.

There were pounds of weed wrapped and stacked on the end of the table. Mark was breaking it down to ounces. Watching Mark work, I noticed the box on the floor filled with bags full of weed. I was about to grab a pound of weed, but Deatz sat a large black bag in front of me and a pair of latex gloves. Deatz told me that I needed to break down the bag to group ten pills per set. After I got the gloves on, I picked up a pill and it looked more like candy than a pill.

From behind me, Deatz yelled "That's ecstasy, you know what they are, right? You asked for fifty of them." Honestly, I had never seen ecstasy before. I had heard of it and from what I knew of it, it was used by people going to Rave club. Something about the techno music and ecstasy. It seemed as it was becoming more popular. I got to know a lot about ecstasy as I counted out each hit. Deatz felt like talking about what he knew about it. He reminded me of someone who just learned about something and has been waiting to tell someone.

It took me over half an hour to get everything done, and another twenty minutes to get out of the house. As I walked out, Deatz told me to come back on Wednesday to get everything I needed and handed me an ounce.

After running around all day and not eating anything, I was hungry. Since that was the only thought on my mind, I went home to see what was to eat. While I drove out of Fostoria, I was already thinking about going out with Sara and our friends. I knew Duke was excited to see Jenny for a real date. It made me chuckle to think about how Duke would act this time. He had calmed down by the time we left yesterday. As I wondered and hoped that I get some alone time with Sara, I noticed a cop behind me with his lights on.

All I could think was, what did this ass hole want. I pulled over and he walked up to my driver's side door. He stood straight as if there was a stick down his back. He asked me if I knew why I was being pulled over. Being a cocky kid, I was quick to reply with "If I say why you pulled me over, would that not be me admitting to guilt? With that in mind, I will say that you pulled me over to accuse me of something I did not do."

He did not find it funny and said I was going seventy in a fifty-five mile per hour. I reached for my driver's license and the registration. As I did, I grabbed a pen and paper, then started writing down his badge number and name. He did not even look at my license or registration but focused on me writing down his information. That seemed to really piss him off. He said in an angry voice "Why are you writing down my name and badge number? What are you planning?" As he finished asking his question, he was bent down to be at eye level with me. I was hoping that he was not on the up and up, so I told him that I would be calling his station to get the rest of his information in case I need to get a lawyer involved.

He lectured me about how I should respect him because he was an "Officer of the Law". After going on, he gave me a verbal warning and telling me if he pulls me over again, he will make me regret it. I said thank you and wrote down what he said. That even pissed him off more and he walked away. I know that I was going sixty and he wanted to have a power trip. Cops like him tend to be the ones that you would read in the news. He would most likely be getting arrested for abuse of power or something worse than what most people do.

I got home shortly after that, but I timed it just right. When walking in the house, the phone in the kitchen was ringing. When I answered it, it was Sara. She seemed to be so full of energy and she asked me if I could invite Mark to come with us. I knew she wanted to play matchmaker again since it seemed that Duke and Jenny would be working out. Since I wanted to make her happy, I promised to call him. We talked for another ten minutes or so. Finally, she let me go after saying she would meet me at Jenny's place.

I called Mark's house and while it was ringing, I stretched the cord attached to the handset. I wanted to look into the refrigerator. When I reached for some leftover lasagna someone answered the phone. It was Jay and he sounded like he was crying. First, I asked if everything was OK, but the little shit answered me with a cocky low brow comment. I let it go and asked him to talk to Mark. He yelled and a few moments later, Mark got on the phone. I made it quick by saying "Mark if you don't have any plans, get over here. Sara wants you to meet a girl and make a group of our bowling outing."

Mark told me that he would be over and we could ride over together. That was fine because I would have time to eat. He hung up and I put a plate in the microwave. While I waited, I called Sara and told her Mark was coming. She hung up without a word. That left me to wait for Mark and eat my mom's lasagna.

CHAPTER FOUR

THERE WASN'T MUCH TO say about our group bowling. It was a good time and we all goofed off a lot. The people in the next lane seemed to be upset with us, but we had fun. Duke was happy that he got a good kiss as he put it, and Mark got along with the Heather girl that Sara brought with her. As for Sara and me, we did our normal joking around with each other and trying to be as close as we could. Afterward, we dropped the girls off at Jenny's house while Duke, Mark, and I went back to my place.

For the next month, the six of us would hang out together. That was till one day when Mark and I were waiting for a guy who said he wanted to buy a nice quantity of weed and acid from us. Mark and I had made a nice little network of about six teens who sold better than we could do. We both were amazed by how much we had done in a month. Deatz even took notice of what we had done and wanted to sit down with us.

I checked the time and saw that this guy was fifteen minutes late. Mark was not happy as this guy was very vague about how much he wanted. We joked that his idea of a lot was a dime bag and two tabs of acid.

Mark said that he did not think he wanted to see Heather anymore. He was in the middle of explaining why he did not like her but liked hanging out with the rest of us. When the guy finally did show up, I was explaining to Mark that he did not have to see some girl to be able to hang out with us. Halfway through, that guy tried to interrupt me.

I hate rude people and he already was rude by being late.

Now he was acting as though our conversation did not matter. Once I finished what I was saying to Mark, I went over to the guy. It was easy to see that he had never done anything like this before. His hands were gripped tight and he had his weight on a foot that was a bit back. He looked as if he was preparing to be hit or start a fight. Noticing this, I got about two feet in front of him and asked if he was trying to be rude.

His voice cracked a bit when he said: "I am here just to buy something. Do you have what I want or not?" Mark started to laugh behind me and walked up to us. I let Mark talk to him since he seemed more in the mood for it. Mark said "I have two questions before we start, what is your name and what do you want? We were told that you wanted a lot, but that is not a quantity, that's a descriptor." The guy said his name was Jimmy. With that, we started to walk away from him. He yelled and ran up between us and our car, asking where we were going. This time I took the lead by telling him that we knew his name was Dan and he hasn't done a lot of sales.

You could see the embarrassment on his face. Dan tried to backtrack to get us to stay. I had a bad feeling about this guy, as he did not seem to be on the level. I asked Mark to get my bag and then I told Dan to get his money. As I kind of expected, he pulled out a knife and yelled at me to give him everything we had. Mark started to laugh again from the car. He was laughing because we had nothing more than a quarter bag on us. Mark suggested that we did not bring anything since this Dan guy was unknown to us.

Mark might have found it funny because he called it, but I was on the other end of the spectrum. This piss ant wanted to threaten us after being late and then interrupting me. I walked up closer to him where we were in arms reach of each other. Standing there looking him in the eyes, I asked what he was going to do. Dan stop threatening, but it sounded more like he was pleading. There is a simple rule I was taught years ago when I pulled a knife on my father, Cameron. That rule was, if you pull a weapon on someone, you better be ready to use it or be ready for a hell of an ass whooping. I backhanded Dan across his face. He was shocked that it was going down like this. Most people would act differently to having a knife pulled on them. However, I had been through more than most people my age.

Dan stepped back and rubbed his face while still pointing the knife towards me. I stepped forward and this time I kicked him like I was trying to kick a field goal. When my foot landed back to the ground, Dan had dropped to the ground as well. By this time, Mark was walking up and said that he believed Dan had learned his lesson. I was not sure of that, and I wanted to make sure that he and others knew not to mess with us. Then I let my anger get the best of me. I sat on his chest and punched him in the face until Mark pulled me off. Dan was beaten and bruised, but nothing that wouldn't be gone in a couple days.

When Mark let go of me, I slowly walked back and picked up a broken piece of a brick laying a few feet away from Dan. Mark freaked out and yelled at me. I did not look back to Mark, but I bent over and grabbed Dan by the head and turned it to the side. In a single swipe, I pushed a pointed edge of the brick from the side of his eye to his ear. After I stood over him watching Dan cry while his tears and blood ran down his face, I felt bad. I knew that I went too far and I could not change what I did. My stomach started to bunch up and I felt shivers running down my back.

Mark came up to me and pushed me into the passenger seat of my car. While I sat there, Mark went back and got Dan's wallet out of his pants to look at it. Then he dropped it in front of Dan as Mark walked back to the car. He climbed through the window and we drove away.

A few blocks down the road, I started to come back to my senses and my stomach was back to normal. The only thing I could say was "Did I really just do that or was that in my head?" Mark pointed to the broken piece of brick I was still holding with blood covering one edge.

I dropped the brick on the floor and kicked it through the hole in my floorboards. Mark said "His name is Daniel Horn and he is from Fostoria. I will deal with any friends he has since I know the people there. So how are you doing? I never saw you get that carried away." I could not believe that I had done that. I told Mark and myself that I couldn't go that far again. I think Mark was relieved by that. For me, I was not so relieved since I just realized that my anger could push me to do some horrible things.

While we drove back to Mark's house, I stared at my hands as we discussed what we had to get done for the guys we were supplying. I could not help focusing on how red my knuckles were. My left hand even had a cut with a little bit of blood coming out. I wiped off the blood and looked up. I did not realize we had parked in front of Mark's house already. Mark had already gotten out of the car.

There was not much time before I realized where we were and Mark came running out of his house. Given how fast he was moving, I had to think something was wrong. I was right, too. Mark asked me to roll up the windows and let's get into his car. I understood that he liked his car better, just because the driver door is not welded shut. I figured he had a reason to be in a hurry, so I switched cars and we were off.

"Are you going to tell me what is going on?" My question was not a tough one, but it had Mark in a frantic state. About six blocks later, he told me that Deatz called his house saying he wanted to see both of us. All I could think was that our luck for that day had run out and when Deatz called, it could not be good.

Pulling across the street and parking, I saw Deatz was sitting on the porch. He was wearing some multi-colored long sleeve shirt. It would be best described as something a rainbow puked on. After getting past the shirt, I noticed he was smiling.

Mark and I were confused about this and did not waste any time to get up to him. By the time our first foot stepped on the porch, he said "You have no idea how happy I am. Let's go in so I can explain better and give you both a nice gift."

"Well shit, these are your top guys? They don't look old enough to shave." This was what we heard when we walked into the house, from a guy that looked to be in his late twenties. I had never seen him before, but he acted like we were friends the moment the door closed behind us. Deatz did not even seem to pay attention to what was going on and walked into his kitchen. The stranger told us who he was and that he is the one that delivers Deatz's supplies. What I found interesting, was when he mentioned a guy named John. I had heard Deatz say that same name before and I got the feeling that John scared Deatz. This made me want to know more about this John character, so I asked.

As I was being told about John and how he is a boss in a New York crime family, Deatz walked back into the front room to join us. Without warning, Deatz tossed a small rectangular object to both Mark and me. Mark got hit in the face while mine hit my stomach. I was not as distracted as Mark, so I noticed it had a small screen and was in some kind of clip that it slid into. The stranger looked at what I had in my hand and told me that it was a nicer pager than he had.

Neither Mark nor I knew anything about pagers. Deatz told us that we need to call him at the number he pages us whenever he sends a page. Mark looked at me and had the same confused look on his face as I must have had. I figured Mark would not ask, so I did. "What is a pager and what happens when you page us?" It must have seemed like a stupid question to those guys because they both laughed. I felt kind of stupid once it was explained.

While we were smoking a joint, they told us how well we had been doing. Some people had taken notice of how we had increased the need for supplies. I guessed that Deatz said something about us. I would learn later that being known is not always a good thing.

We learned that John in New York wanted to know why there had been an increase in the orders. Considering that Deatz did not like to discuss his dealers to anyone, I did not think he was too forthcoming about Mark and me.

Mark and I decided that we needed to go, till the stranger started talking again. I had a bad feeling when the stranger looked at me and said "Deatz, do you remember when you met John? You were so nervous and it did not help that John just finished teaching a guy why loyalty was important? I could not believe that John's hands were as red as your guy's hands are now. That guy never shorted a payment again." The stranger kept looking at me as if that was meant for me. Deatz looked at the guy with anger filling his face. I took it that the story of him meeting John was not meant to be shared.

I did not feel comfortable any longer, so I got up to leave. Mark stood by the door looking as he wanted to get out of there in a hurry, too. We said goodbye and walked out the door. I thought we had gotten away till Deatz came to his door and said my name. When I turned around, Deatz asked me about my hands. I explained the event that happened earlier and Deatz wanted to know the kid's name. Mark jumped in and told Deatz that we could handle it. Deatz told us to keep the pagers with us and walked back into his house.

Mark grabbed my shirt and pulled me off the porch. We ended back at his house. We sat on the porch and smoked a few cigarettes while talking about what had happened. Mark told me he had seen Deatz talk to John before. The details Mark gave me, made John seem even scarier than I had figured. I wondered how it would be to meet this John.

Neither of us wanted to talk much after that. We exchanged pager numbers that we found written on the back of the pager and then I left to go home to rest.

It seemed to already be about dinner time and I had not eaten since breakfast. I was starving and could only think about eating. That must be why I did not notice Duke's car parked on the street in front of my house. When I walked in, Duke was sitting at the dining room table, while Sara and Jenny were helping my mom cook. I did not remember if it was planned that we all were to meet at my place. When I looked at Duke, he shrugged his shoulders. Sara noticed I was there and turned around with a smile. She came over to kiss me but would not touch me with her hands. They were covered in a mixture of what looked like flour and dough.

Finally, I gave in and asked what was going on. Sara had been to my house a few times. Duke was over enough that my step-dad joked with him about giving him a key to the house. Sara and Duke had not been here at the same time, and neither had Jenny, so I was confused.

Jenny answered me by saying that she and Sara got to talking about who made a better dinner. It was between my mom and Duke's dad. This led them to my house where my mom was teaching them how to make a Reuben loaf from scratch.

I still was confused but decided to sit down and enjoy having them over, plus I loved Reuben loaf. While I began to relax, Duke asked what happened to my hands. As was my luck, my mom walked in and heard the question. She looked at my bruised and cut knuckles then came over picking up my hands. I was not sure if she was worried or upset, but I watched what I said because I did not want my mom upset. At that time, I did not fear anyone other than my mom.

I made up a story about me helping a girl out from being with a very aggressive guy. The story seemed to make everyone calm down and go back to what they were doing.

That was everyone except Duke. He gave me a sign to say

that we should go smoke and we went outside. Duke didn't even wait till my cigarette was lit when he asked what happened. I told him about what that Dan guy did and how I gave him a cut across his face. I did not think of it as being exciting or anything, but Duke thought so. He kept asking questions with excitement in his voice. After we finished smoking, I changed the subject and Duke took a hit.

The rest of the evening was spent with us all eating dinner and talking about all sorts of things. Around eight I took Sara home while Duke took Jenny home. Along the way, I decided to stop on the side of a country road. Sara and I smoked a small joint and laid on my hood. We laid there looking up at the stars and helped each other. It went that way for about an hour when Sara told me she had to get going. She had to do something with her parents the following day. As much as I wanted to keep her in my arms, I took her the rest of the way home. Once she walked through her doorway and closed the door, my night was over.

CHAPTER FIVE

SOME DAYS HAD PASSED and I had been working on a plan with a guy named Steve. He was a senior and most likely the smartest person in our school. He would talk with me because he didn't think he'd get to go to college after high school. Steve wanted to, but his dad was hooked on pain killers and drank like a fish since he had gotten hurt at the forgery. Steve refused to leave his younger sister alone with his father, so he chose to stay close. From what Steve said, he would like to take classes at Bowling Green State University since he could drive there daily. He just needed to come up with the money to pay for it. That is why we were making a plan to benefit both of us.

During his lunch period, I met with him to see what we could do. I don't know how he knew what he did about drugs and how to push them, but I was impressed. He must have spent some time figuring out what he wanted to do. What he needed from me was an advance of the product. He made a comment about how he heard what I do to people that cross me, and it made me chuckle. From what he told me, he would make us both good money. I agreed and told him that I would get him everything he needed in two days.

Steve was happy that I was advancing him three thousand dollars' worth of product. After that, he pointed out that my book bag was making some sounds. I did not even notice until he said something, but it was the pager Deatz had given me and I guessed it was Deatz calling. My problem was, I did not know if it was or not. I just saw a number on the screen and I had no idea what his phone number was. There was only one way to find out. I called the number from the payphone outside the lunchroom in the hallway.

It was not Deatz's home number, but it was Deatz. He sounded like he was at a payphone too. Once he knew it was me, he told me he had something I had to do. When I asked what benefit I got from running his errands, he clearly said, "First you will come to my place and pick up money from me. Then you will get to Fremont to meet someone. I will give you more details when you get here. As for what you get out of it, you should feel lucky. You get two things, the first is that I am not going to break any of your bones for being an ass hole. The other is your pricing. I will give you a better cut on your price, but don't you ever talk to me again like that. Do you understand?"

I realized I had overstepped my boundaries for the last time and I always kept that in mind. Before we hung up, Deatz told me that I had to come right after I got out of school. Just as I grabbed my bag off the floor to get to class, I remembered I had to work my real job. It seemed pointless to keep doing it. I was making more in one or two deals than I made in a month punching out the copper from a small, dirty motor. This made it a clear choice of what I had to do. I dug in my bag looking for a quarter.

While I was kneeling and my head almost inside my book bag, Sara came up and put her foot in the center of my butt cheeks. She laughed so damn hard when I jumped, I hit my shoulder on the payphone and tripped over my bag. "What the hell are you doing? You scared the shit out of me." As I yelled that to Sara, a teacher that I always called Boogie happened by and was the same teacher who hated me. He gave me a line about watching my language or I would be sent to the principal's office. The idiot did not notice that the principal was right there trying not to laugh at me.

When Sara stop laughing and I had everything picked up

from my bag, we gave each other a little kiss. I explained to Sara that I needed a quarter to call off work. I noticed that Sara was feeling around in her purse while she was asking questions about why I was calling off. I tried to let her know that I had to meet up with Deatz. Then Sara got me excited when she pulled her hand out of her purse and looked at her palm smiling.

It did not make me as happy as she was when she showed me an earring she held in her hand. She told me how she thought she lost it in my car, but now she was happy to have the pair again. My face must have told her that I was not impressed and she turned where the principal was. "Principal Simmons, do you have a quarter? Scott needs to call his job and I want to see if his boss yells at him." That made the principal laugh and she walked over while reaching in her pocket. When Principal Simmons got to us, I was standing and had slung my bag onto my back.

With a hand held out that was full of change, Principal Simmons put her arm around Sara and gave her a little squeeze. While they stood there being buddies, the principal told Sara that guys like me need to have a good woman. She added "Guys like Scott are smart but will get themselves in trouble. A good girl like you will help him on the right track." Sara being the girl she was, made comments about that is why she gives me a hard time. They had a few good quips at my expense, but I let them have their fun. As I dialed the scrap yard, I heard them going on making jokes.

On the second ring, the owner answered the phone. First, there was a loud cough followed with the sound of the person taking a puff off a cigar. I knew that moment it was Mr. Kissiner the owner of the scrap yard. He was a tough guy with a sense of humor that made most people cringe. If you did not know this before calling, you would know when he answered the phone. Mr. Kissiner exhaled heavily into the phone while saying "Who the hell is this?"

I learned quickly when working at the scrapyard not to

answer him weakly. It took one day of work to learn that and from there on, I talked to Mr. Kissiner as if I'd known him for years, and you just did not curse unless it was fitting. I guess that is why when I started to talk, my principal got a strange look on her face.

It was a simple conversation. I started with "Sir; this is Scott. I can't come in today and this time it has nothing to do with the pretty little thing I am seeing. I just have a last—minute engagement to deal with." At first, I thought Mr. Kissiner was fine with it. He changed my mind with his response. He said "That is fine, I was going to invite you for dinner anyways to tell you this, but I will save you the time. The daytime guy is looking for more hours and he gives us a higher output. So, if you need a reference, let us know, other than that, good luck." I did not get a chance to answer him when he hung up the phone.

By this time Principal Simmons was walking away and Sara stood there looking at me. When I hung up the phone, I told Sara that I don't have to worry about stripping copper anymore. I think she felt worse about it than I did. That was till I explained that it was between me and a grown man trying to pay bills. We both knew how hard it was for some people, so I didn't take it personally. On top of that, I was making more in a few deals then if I worked for a month at the scrap yard.

With everything handled, I started to walk Sara to her next class. While we walked down the hallway, Sara said she wanted to come with me after school to wherever I was going. Normally I would love that, but I did not want Deatz to see her. I could also tell that she did not want to go home.

Sara gave me a kiss when we got to her class as she headed in. Hating to see her feeling down, I grabbed her hip to stop her. When Sara turned back to me, I told her that I will figure out something. That is all it took to make her cheer up and I had a couple of hours to figure it out. It was not until I got to my car and Sara was standing there when I figured out how I could make sure

Deatz did not see her. When we got in my car, Sara asked what we are doing.

It was about time that I explained how far I was in with the drug trade so she would understand what was going on. By the time I finished, she said that she is OK with everything, as long as I did not do the drugs I was pushing. I agreed except for smoking weed, since I enjoyed that and it didn't hurt anything. Now that I did not have to worry about hiding anything from Sara, I told her that I had to meet with Deatz. She told me she would wait at the pizza shop next to Deatz's house while I was at his place. From that point, we joked about my criminal empire and how she was a mob princess. These jokes went all the way to Fostoria. Then Sara asked a serious question about the dangers I might face. I honestly did not think about being in any danger, but then again, I did not know what Deatz wanted me to do.

Of course, I told her that I was in no danger, but I had faced a little with that Dan guy. Now Deatz had Mark and me on call and we did not know what for. Sara did not need to know any of these things. I could see that she was worried that I possibly could be in danger.

If she knew what had happened with Dan, and my own concern with whatever Deatz had me doing, she would be freaking out. It was a quiet drive for the last few city blocks to the pizza shop. When we got there, Sara jumped out of the car saying how hungry she was. I gave her a fifty and told her I would be a quick as I could.

Not having a single concern, Sara went in for pizza and to wait for me. I wish I could have been able to stay with her. Instead, I pulled my car in front of Deatz's house and went in. Of course, Deatz got a good laugh when his dogs tackled me. After he got his dogs off me and stopped laughing at me, we got to why he wanted me to come over. He dropped a paper grocery bag in my lap and handed me a Colt .380 ACP.

Looking into the bag, it was full of twenties and tens. Before I was able to ask a question, Deatz told me about a guy who was coming through from New York. The sack of cash was for me to exchange for two large duffel bags full of drugs. The gun was in case the guy tried to cross me or did anything out of line. This did not lessen the concerns I was having with needing a gun. I was always taught that you only point a gun at what you plan to shoot and you better be ready to shoot.

To add to all the odd events I felt I was in, Deatz gave me his house key. As he put the key in my hand, he told me the command to have his dogs not attack when entering. I could just picture the headline on the paper. It would say "Teen mauled to death as entering a house carrying drugs." I am sure my mom and stepdad would love that.

I had enough and did not want to add to this, so I began to leave. Deatz stopped me as I reached for the door and told me two things. The first was he would be going to Chicago with Mark after I left, but they would be back in the morning. The second item was that the next time I come around, I better not bring a girl, even if I was dropping her off at the pizza shop. He let me know that I would suffer a lot of pain if I did not listen to him about my girlfriend. With that, I was out the door carrying the bag with the gun hidden in the back of the waistband of my pants.

I did not waste any time and got back to the pizza shop parking lot. I told her not to walk over to my car because I didn't want Deatz to see her. I guess that was stupid of me.

As I backed out from moving my car from the street to the parking lot, a total of maybe ten yards, Mark pulled up and parked where my car sat a moment ago. Mark saw me and yelled to me for my attention. We met each other halfway and talked about what was going on.

I gave a quick rundown of what I had to do and how it sounded like he was going to Chicago. Mark said he already knew about Chicago. He was told that they were going to get our weekly orders filled by some guy there. From the little I knew about the guy in New York, I didn't think he would be forgiving if he found out about the Chicago connection. That's why I stressed to Mark that he didn't give his name out unless he has to. Not knowing what game Deatz was playing, I didn't want Mark to get wrapped up and hurt. Plus, Mark and I were just getting our business going, as I had hoped. We were making enough money that I was close to being able to buy a new car. Mark nodded and we went our ways with a final "be safe, talk with you later."

Sara was already next to my car waving to Mark and smiling. When Sara and I got in the car, she said that she called her mom and things were better, so she could go home. I figured it was a short distance out of the way, but it's better than having her with me at the exchange. If this guy beat me there, it would be OK. On our way, she reached to the back seat and grabbed a slice of pizza she had put back there and gave it to me.

"So, I am guessing that I am not supposed to know about the bag of money back there?" She followed that comment up with a cocky smile. I told her that I had to buy this time instead of sell. That was all she needed to know. It was another ten minutes of her making jokes again about how I am part of the drug cartel. Sara jokingly tried to figure out how low I was on the chain. When we got to her house, it was a kiss and a goodbye with her taking the pizza with her.

Now I had to get to the exchange and hope that everything went smoothly. I drove down country roads going as fast as I could with my beat-up Firebird. I made good time when I got on Route twenty outside of Fremont. From there it was only a few minutes till I got off on fifty-three. After that, I only had to find the trucker parking area that was across the street from a motel called Deluxe Motel. I understood why this guy wanted to meet there, it was hidden and off the main road.

I had to go to a gas station and ask where it was. Oddly enough, Mick was there filling up his car. When I told him that I was looking for the motel, he knew right where it was and told me that I was only one turn away. I had to go back towards Fremont and make a right at the first turn. The motel was down the street and Mick said I couldn't miss it. He stopped me before driving off and asked if he could add a few ounces to his last request. Since I didn't see an issue, I told him that it would be taken care of. Then I was back on the road.

CHAPTER SIX

I DID NOT WAIT LONG when the guy showed up. When he came into the gravel lot, he pulled up next to me and asked if I was Scott Bearman or Mark Himlee. I figured it was a good sign that he knew who was coming. As I started to tell him that I am Scott Bearman, I must have not answered quickly enough to suit him as he was reaching under a shirt on his passenger seat. I was pretty sure that he was going for his gun. I repeated myself and started to reach for the colt that Deatz gave me.

"Listen, before either of us do something, I don't want to get lead poisoning and I don't think you want to either. We can make our exchange and get what we came for or make a scene." I don't know where that came from, but once I said it, he got out of his car and put his gun away as I did mine. Getting the tension out of the way and not having any more concern about being shot, we started to talk and get to know each other.

He opened the trunk of his car and pulled out the bags. This guy didn't seem to care much about the cops or anyone else seeing us. He put the bags on my hood and opened them up for me to look inside. I rummaged through to see if everything was in there. Deatz told me what to expect. There was no way I would count it on the spot. It dawned on me how much the drug trade was based on trust. I trusted him enough to accept that all the drugs were there. He trusted me enough to take the bag of cash and believe I wasn't shorting him. We both finished the exchange and put the bags away.

Since we were done, I was going to leave and drop everything off at Deatz's place before calling it a day. Instead, this guy wanted to talk more. He lit a cigarette and sat down on the hood of my car. For some reason, he looked at me as if I insulted him by not joining him. There only seemed to be one option for now, so I sat on the hood of my car with him. He offered me a cigarette from his pack. It was not menthol, so I took it. It was some cheap brand and tasted like crap, but I smoked it. Playing nice and all helps move things forward.

While we talked, I was told that he was asked by John to find out more about Mark and me. I made sure I never mentioned any of my friends or Sara. I also did not want my friends and family to know about these people in New York. It was interesting to learn that the guy I was talking with dealt with the transportation of the product. He managed all logistics through the Midwest and to other gangs or mobsters. He had made a trip out of his way to meet me. We chatted about thirty minutes before we were finished. He said I would be the only acceptable person to make the exchanges other than Deatz.

He slid off my car and went to his car. He reached into his backseat and pulled out a revolver. This was not what I expected, and I quickly reached for my gun, which was still at my back. I would have pulled it, but he opened up the cylinder and held it out for me to take.

It was a Smith & Wesson forty-five ACP revolver. It was a nice looking gun and I could only imagine how nice it must shoot. I held it back out to him, but he was holding a box of ammo. Turns out, he was giving me the gun. Hearing his reason for giving me the gun, I could not help to wonder how I got here. I went from some low-level dealer to someone who had to carry guns with me. This guy stressed that he likes Smith &Wesson forty-five because he knew from personal experience that it will shoot through a door and take the person out. He joked about how John hates to see anything happen to his future investments.

He got in his car after that and drove away. I didn't know what to make of the whole episode. As far as I was concerned, I had to get the drugs to Deatz's house

I waited until after he left and got on the road as well. Even though it had started getting dark, I did not realize what time it was. This whole trip took longer than I figured. It was almost seven and I was expected to be home in about half an hour. To add to it, I was hungry and did not want to miss dinner. There was a rule in my mom's house that if you want a hot dinner, be on time.

The drive from Fremont to Fostoria took about thirty minutes. When I came to Deatz's house, there was someone sitting on his porch. Instead of stopping to see who it was, I drove on by. Taking a chance that the person was friendly was not a gamble I was willing to take. I felt Deatz would understand.

It was not long before I was home with a lot of drugs in my trunk. That night, I got to enjoy a personal joke. I had to park on the street in front of my house and behind the town's chief of police's car. I walked into the house as the mayor and chief were trying to talk my step-dad into joining the city council. They both greeted me as I walked in. My step-dad pointed at a plate of food and said that I should eat before it gets any colder.

It was interesting to listen to them talk about how they wanted my step-dad to help improve the town. They thought he could help attract and keep younger families to move into town. The funniest thing was when the police chief said he had made sure drugs were staying out of our small town. I could only wonder what he would say if he knew how wrong he was.

I got bored with listening to them talk, and finished eating before going out for a cigarette. I don't know why, but the chief came out to smoke with me. He leaned against my car with me and made a comment about not being allowed to smoke in the house. After that and getting his cigarette lit, he decided to talk to me. He talked about all the things he did in our small town when he was my age. I believed that he felt that they were tall stories and I would be impressed. The only interesting story he told me was about the first time he smoked weed. He liked to keep telling me how it was the seventies and a different time.

I went into the house to end the conversation. It was not long after that, both guests left. Leaving just my mom, step-dad, and me. We all called it a night, but I could not sleep very well. I kept waking up looking out my bedroom window that allowed me to see my car on the street. By five-thirty in the morning, I said the hell with it and got completely up.

After getting dressed and around, I walked in the kitchen where my step-dad was sipping on his coffee. It caught me off guard seeing him there. I never realized how early he went to work and he had questions on why I was up too. I did not want to lie, but I was not going to tell the complete truth. I don't believe he would think it is a good thing if I said I had to drop off several bags of drugs and let some dogs out.

He was OK with hearing that I was going to let dogs out for someone out of town. I grabbed my car keys and before I got out the door, I was stopped and handed a travel mug full of coffee. That black coffee warmed me up and woke me up. From that day on I always had a cup of coffee to start the day. Most of the coffee was gone by the time I pulled in front of Deatz's house.

I was not wasting any time. These drugs had kept me up all night and I was happy to get rid of them. I did not even think about the dogs being trained guard dogs when I went to enter the house. After turning the key to the front door and opening it, the two big dogs were not happy to see me. The dogs came running towards me. They stopped in the middle of the living room. I thought I would be a chew toy when I said the phrase Deatz told me and they did not back down. Instead, they started to take steps towards me. I started to feel I could see their teeth through the darkness that filled the house.

Finally, I yelled "persido!, persido!, FOR GOD SAKES persido!" and that did the trick. Both dogs sat down in front of me whimpering. Walking the rest of the way in, those dogs ran up to me wanting to get some attention from me. Of course, I gave it to them, then took them to the back yard to do whatever they had to do. This was not something I was asked to do, but I was not going to let the dogs suffer.

In fact, the scare those dogs gave me, made me want a smoke. So I went out with them and dropped the bags in the kitchen on our way through. It was so relaxing that I could have fallen asleep right there, even with the chill I felt from the wind. I might of too, but one of the dogs nudged me with his nose. I took that as a signal that they wanted in and we went back inside.

Locking everything back up and turning off the lights, I was about to leave. Instead, I flopped down on the same chair I sat in when I first come inside the house. This time, I did doze off and was awakened by the sound of the dogs growling again. Except it was not at me. The door opened and before I saw who was coming, I looked to see if I had either gun on me. I didn't, but realized I didn't need them when I heard Deatz yell persido.

Looking at the clock, I saw that it was just after seven in the morning. Deatz quickly noticed me. He first yelled at Mark to set the bags in the kitchen while looking at me. Then he addressed me and he definitely was not thrilled to see me in his house. Once he gave me a moment to explain, I told him about the guy on the porch. I kept saying how I just showed up and also let the dogs out, and he seemed to accept that. He also thanked me for taking care of the dogs.

Mark came in and joined us after that. Mark seemed as if he had a lot on his mind. He looked as though he was tired too. I felt it best not to push Mark at the moment. We could talk about everything later. I currently had to get out the door and to school.

If I could just get Deatz to sum up what he was trying to tell me, I would have been out the door.

Instead, he wanted to discuss a plan that would have me start doing all the exchanges with John's guys. I asked what changed and what kind of discounts Mark and I were getting. Deatz looked at me as I was annoying him with my concerns. This went on for another fifteen minutes of him saying what he wanted me to do without answering what was in it for me. It ended up pissing me off and I got up to walk out, but Deatz stopped me, demanding I let him finish.

What I said to him could have gone two ways as I saw it. The first was he would give answers to my question about what I was getting out of it. The other option would end with me having some broken bones or worse. Either way, I said; "I don't work for you or free. What you want me to do could cost me years in prison. If I am taking a risk for you, I expect a payoff. Till then, I am done and I can find product from someone else."

I turned back to the door and was pushed against the wall and the door. Mark yelled to Deatz asking him not to hurt me. Deatz punched me a few times in the side of the ribs and kneed me in my leg to make sure I fell. He let go of me and with the pain in my leg, I dropped down to one of my knees.

"You cocky bastard, do you think you would walk out after talking to me like that? I warned you and you still tried it. Sit down and we will work out a deal or I will finish kicking your ass and throw you out to lay in the street." I understood that Deatz needed to show Mark that "his people" could not get away with it. I accepted his offer to discuss how we would move forward, as though I had a choice.

We made an agreement that Mark and I got everything at ten percent above Deatz's cost. We would also learn the business from him. This allowed us all to make more money. I was very happy with this agreement. Now Mark and I could figure out how to grow our profit on what we were already doing. I would not say it, but I was thinking how this would allow us to take over.

More to my delight was that I had become the person dealing with the supplier. I would not ever tell anyone that I was happy about this, but I had already started to think about how to use it to my advantage. Mark still seemed as if he was concerned about something.

I did not have time to wait to talk to Mark afterward. I got up and shook Deatz's hand and before I walked out the door, I told Mark we would meet up after school. I saw him give me the thumbs up as I was walking out the door. I tried to get to school as fast as I could, but I needed some coffee first. I was still tired and a caffeine pick-me-up would be helpful.

Stopping at a small blue gas station on County Road, I got a mocha drink. It was nothing more than caffeinated hot cocoa. No matter what it was, I liked to think it would give me the kick in the butt to get going. Trying to get in my car with a hot drink, I was surprised by Jay Himlee. I called him over to talk.

He said he was walking to school since his brother did not come home to give him a ride. I figured I was already going to be late, so I told him to get in and I drove him so he would not be late too.

Jay seemed happy not to have to walk the rest of the way. From how Mark told me he was trying to make sure Jay made something of himself. It took me off guard when he said he would be dropping out of school when he turns sixteen. For the short drive, I listened to him tell me how he was barely passing, then how people like him never get out of Fostoria. I did not want to tell him, but he was right. He was not smart and with his family, he would most likely sell drugs, be on them, or both. Either way, I would bet that he lived, died, and would be buried in Fostoria.

I pulled up to the school and as he got out, he asked me not to say anything to Mark. Jay had been an ass every time I had seen him before so I wasn't sure why he decided to open up to me. I promised him, but it was not for his benefit that I would not tell Mark. It would kill Mark to know that his brother had already decided and accepted his fate.

This time as I drove down the road, I did not stop till I got to my school and it took time to find a parking spot when I did get there. Walking towards the front entrance, I heard the bell ring for the first period. That meant I had no choice but to stop at the principal's office and receive an approval pass. It had always been easier when Sara was with me. She would walk up to the girl behind the counter, say something and they would giggle. Then we would be on our way.

The front counter girl did not find me as charming, but she remembered that Sara and I are a thing. With that, she stopped herself from being short with me. That was as far as she and I were going to get. As I told her for the third time that I was late because of car problems, Principal Simmons came out and took over. I figured she heard me getting frustrated and wanted to put an end to it.

Principal Simmons had me come into her office and sit down. Any time I was in the principal's office, I never had a good experience. I hoped it would be different this time when she pulled out a pass. Instead of just giving me a pass, she insisted I tell her why I was really late. I told her as close to the truth as I could, starting with reminding her of the quarter I got from her to call my work.

Once she remembered, I told her how I lost my job. Since then, I had been working for a guy out of Fostoria with sales and product planning. She seemed interested in my explanation of what I was doing. I finished it off by saying how I met with that guy and discussed how I would be able to start my own business and that he would be training me.

I must have been more believable then I thought. Principal

Simmons told me that she would be willing to work with me on changing class schedules. She wanted to help me go to work. I was getting all sorts of praise about how she knew I was able to do big things. Only then did she finally write me the approval pass.

The end of the first-period bell rang as I was on my way to class. Not having to hurry to my first class, I went to find Sara and Duke. I found them in the hallway between my locker and Sara's locker. The three of us would use each other's lockers to save from carrying so many books. When I got to them, they were shocked to see me and started to question me about where I was. It was best to get to them up to date. The nice thing about talking with them, I could openly tell them everything.

"Now wait till you hear this. I talked with Deatz this morning and I made a deal that will make me more money. I also now have a direct connection to his supplier. I think we are going to have plenty of money soon." Duke was the first to reply with "What do you mean we? You are doing all this work and taking the risk, what do you think we are going to do?" Then Sara added with asking "Are you putting yourself in more danger?" Before I got to answer, they started to discuss it between the two of them.

They did not seem to be focusing on me. That was, till I put a hand on each of their shoulders. We did not have a lot of time left before the next bell rang. I asked if they wanted to join me to go to Mark's after school. They looked at me as though I asked them to stay after school, but they both agreed. Before we got to talk any more, the bell rang. We went on our own way and finished our day.

Once the school day was over, we met at my car in the parking lot. We talked some more while letting everyone get out so we could have an easier drive. When most of the other kids got out, they would rush out of the parking lot and end up sitting in backed up traffic on Route Eleven. While they were trying to get to Route twenty-three, we waited and I decided to tell Duke and Sara about what Principal Simmons told me. I explained about her working my schedule around to be able to do my job. They laughed about that. Whoever thought a school would give someone the ability to leave school early to sell drugs? By the time we finished joking about that, Sara and I got in my car as Duke got into his car. The drive to Fostoria was easy since everyone had scattered enough by that time.

CHAPTER SEVEN

D UKE PASSED A JOINT to Mark, and I passed mine to Sara. A cold breeze was blowing through the opening of the window. I didn't want to wait any longer and asked Mark what happened on his trip with Deatz to Chicago. Mark's face went from looking as he had a good buzz to being sober as a judge. He glanced at Duke and Sara, then back to me. "What do you mean? Why are you talking about Deatz in front of them?" Mark took a hit of the joint to buy himself some time.

I was feeling good with a nice buzz going too. I reminded Mark that they have been around when we had talked about our business before. It was easy to see that Mark did not remember until Sara asked if Mark made the deal with whoever it was in Tiffin. St that point, Mark smiled and coughed while exhaling. "Yeah, I got it done. The guy agreed to only order from us since one of his friends was working with us. I forgot I told you guys about him."

In such a short time, we had built up a nice network, although our profits could have been better. Mark and I agreed that we could make more by keeping the price down and selling more. It was working too. We spent three evenings and part of Saturdays making drop-offs and meeting with the guys in our network. I also liked that we had a network; it made me feel good that I could build something like this at my age.

Once Mark stopped coughing, he told us about how Deatz and he went to Chicago to meet with someone named Santo. Santo was with the drug cartel and promised good quality at better prices. That was compared to what he was getting from

John. It went good from what Mark said. It seemed that Deatz was trying to pull something, but I was too high to care or fully understand it. I figured that Mark and I would try not to get too involved with anything that might piss off John. The few stories I had heard, John scared me and I didn't want to get on his bad side.

Duke decided he was bored with the topic and asked when I was getting a new car. Sara spoke up before I could and said that she wanted to help pick it out. We decided to go look at new cars on Saturday. Sara was very happy with herself, as she adjusted herself to be between my legs and leaned against me.

As for Mark and Duke, they didn't pay any attention to Sara and me after that. I heard one of them say they would be going with Sara and me on Saturday. The rest of their conversation was discussing what cars were faster and more awesome. Awesome was their word.

We hung out till about midnight until Sara realized the time. She jumped up and grabbed me saying that we had to get going. While I was getting up for us to go, I noticed Duke asleep against a stack of clean clothes. I was going to wake him when Mark stopped me. Mark said Duke could sleep at his place and he would wake him up in the morning. I was not going to debate him; Duke drove himself, and I had to get Sara home. We took off and got on the road. I could only imagine what her dad would say. He most likely was passed out drunk, but if he wasn't, it could be interesting for both of us. Since it was past midnight, the roads were empty and very dark. The cloudy night did not allow any moonlight.

If you wanted to see bad luck, we had it when we passed the only car other than us and pulled into Sara's house. When we got out of my car and I started walking Sara to her door, a cop pulled in with his lights on. This guy had a chip on his shoulder and was not used to being in the country at night. The dumb ass pulled in as if he was about to raid a drug house. He got out of his car with one hand holding a flashlight and the other what I assumed was his gun. It was hard to see since he would not come out from behind his car door. I was about to turn around and see what he wanted. That was till he called out "Hey boy, get over here now." I have no respect for rudeness and continued walking Sara the rest of the way to her door. The cop yelled out again with the same command. I took my time and kissed Sara goodnight before I asked her to go inside.

Now I had to deal with this guy. When I walked back to my car and in his general direction, he freaked out and pulled his gun. I was surprised at first, but a moment after, I got myself into the right mindset. I said to the cop, "Are you trying to be rude and dangerous? You call me boy and I sure as hell am not your boy. Then your point a gun at a minor out in the country. I am just happy that you're not too bright." He did not like that and reached for his handcuffs while telling me he was taking me to jail.

I finished walking to my car and told him I was getting a cigarette and reaching in to get one. He started yelling again, telling me to get down on the ground. He took a few steps in my direction, still yelling that I should get on the ground. By then, I had a cigarette lit and took a hit. While he still had the gun pointed at me, I asked what he was arresting me for. He did not have an answer for that, but he did have an answer when I asked if his dash camera was on.

Once he realized that he was being filmed, he started backing up to his car. Now that he started to think, I decided to add to his stress. "Sir, if you had not come in here being rude, I would have talked to you. Now you can leave, or I will be reporting you for threatening a minor with deadly force. You just want to bother us because it's late." Then things got worse as Sara's dad came out in his pajama pants and a thermal shirt. He was stumbling around and yelling as well.

It was a gamble, but I went to him and stopped him from charging the cop. Dealing with two asses was not my idea of a good time and it was not made any better with it being a cold night.

Sara's dad had focused his anger on the cop, so when I put my hands on his chest, he stopped. While he was staring the cop down, he asked what the hell was going on. He was pissed that he was woken up by someone outside yelling. It took some talking to her dad to calm him down. When I did, he told me to get him a cigarette. I could see that the cold air had sobered him up some, at least enough to think and take in what was going on.

I was not going to argue with the man. He had a short temper and he was on edge already, but the cop had his attention. He started talking to the cop when I went in to get his cigarettes. When I walked into the kitchen, Sara's mom was on the phone with the local police. She told me that they were on their way. She handed me his cigarettes. It was a pack of camels unfiltered and they were strong.

When I got back out, the cop and Sara's dad were yelling at each other. The first thing I heard as I went outside was "Get off my property you low life pig." It was followed by "Sir, you are under arrest for disrespecting an officer of the law." That made me laugh. I handed her dad his cigarettes and grabbed one of mine from my pocket. Her dad was shaking his head and I said to the cop, "you are stupid. There is no law like that."

Before anything else was said, more sirens and light came flying down the road. Two cops pulled into the drive. One of the cops was a friend of my mom, the other I knew as well but not personally. The local cop looked at me and said: "Scott, what the hell is going on."

I started to walk towards the local cops till the first cop who followed me into Sara's house pointed his gun at me again. It made my day when I could point to the other cops and they had their guns pointed at him.

From that point, things became a big mess for the first cop from what I found out later. Once the locals had the other guy disarmed and sitting in the back of their car, I was told to go home. Before I turned on my car, I heard Sara's dad telling the local cops that he wanted to press charges. Then my radio drowned out everything. With Def Leppard's Love Bites playing, I got the hell out of there and home as fast as I could.

The next morning, I thought I had gotten away with getting in so late. That was till my mom came into the kitchen while I was having a bowl of cereal. Without looking at me and what I could swear was a smile, she said "You know you're not as quiet as you think you are. You stomp and curse when you bump into stuff. That is not sneaking in, that is as bad as yelling that you are home."

All I could think about was how glad I was that she was not mad. Before my mom asked, I told her about how we lost track of time at a friend's house and the whole mess when I took Sara home. I gave every detailed account of what happened. It upset her that I had a gun pointed at me. I was not going to tell her that it wasn't my first time.

It was easy to see that she was fighting from losing her temper as she called her friend that was on the scene. He must have been next to the phone because my mom finished dialing when she started to talk to him. I finished my cereal and tried to get out the door while she was still on the phone, but as I went for the door, she told me to sit.

When she hung up the phone, she sat in the chair by me and said that her friend will bring the report over. If she had any questions, I better be ready to answer them. With that, she pointed at the door and told me not to be late to school. From the look on her face, I was not going to say anything other than OK. I got out of the house and for the first time in a long time, I made it to school on time and I did not have to rush around.

I found it strange as I walked down the hall. I saw Sara at her locker and taking everything out of it. Everything, but her books and she seemed to be in a hurry. Getting up next to her, I kissed her on the neck just as I had more times than I could count. This time, Sara jumped in fear and screamed. The others in the hallway stopped to look to see what the sound was. When they realized it was Sara and me, they moved on their way after giving us a dirty glance.

"Sara, what's wrong? You seem on edge and you are packing everything up. It looks like you are running away." She grabbed me after I finished talking and started crying while holding me tighter than she ever had. I had a really bad feeling about what was going on. Whatever was going to happen, I squeezed Sara and did not care who walked by. I don't know how long we held each other, but I believe it was her goodbye. She made me think she wanted to feel the goodbye long past when the words were said.

When she let go of me, she said that her mom was in the principal's office getting everything taken care of. Sara went to walk away until I grabbed her wrist and pulled her back to me. I kissed her and during our kiss, a tear fell from her cheek and hit my arm. We parted and she gave me one last quick hug and told me that she will always love me. Sara had made me happy and now I was scared of what was coming.

When the homeroom bell rang, Sara grabbed her bag and ran off. I watched her run down the hall and away from me. I hated to see her go, as there was nothing left to make me happy. She vanished into the crowd and a guy from my home class grabbed my shoulder. He said, "Bearman, let's go, you will be late, and you are already on Mrs. Kindson's shit list." I followed him, but I was lost in my own thoughts.

The rest of the day seemed to pass by while I went through the motions. My mind was laser-focused on what was happening with Sara. What I do remember from that day after I saw Sara, was the drive to Sara's house after school. I did not notice Duke following me till he pulled in behind me. By the time he got out of his car, I was standing in front of the door holding a note that was addressed to me.

The note said that her mom had been waiting for an opening to get away from Sara's dad and take Sara with her. She could not say where they went in case her dad got the note before I did. It sounded like her mom was moving things out slowly over the past few months. Her dad got arrested trying to leave for more beer while the cops were still there. Sara's mom asked the cops to hold him for at least twenty-four hours and explained why.

After she got done telling me about why and how they left, the note got to the part that hurt the most. Sara wrote about how happy she was to be with me and how she believed we could have had a future together. A few memories were mentioned and finally how she knows we will always love each other, even if we can't be together.

When I looked back up from the note, Duke was standing next to me. My face must have said it all because he grabbed me and let me cry without ever saying a word. I don't know how long it took me to straighten myself out, but when I did, Duke suggested that we get out of there. As bad as I was feeling, he pointed out how much anger and pain Sara's dad would have when he got home.

We ended up at an old barn a little bit back from the road. It was hidden by a bunch of trees and had a nice big clearing behind it. During the summer, people throw parties out there. That is how we knew about it.

We sat there talking till eight-thirty at night trying to figure out what happened. I told Duke about the night before and what happened with Sara at her locker. We finally decided that we would never know the whole story. When Duke accepted that I was not going to go do anything crazy, we left, and I went home. I thought Duke wanted to see Jenny and tell her about Sara. I also think he wanted a reason to see her.

I only wanted to go lay in my bed and had all the intention to do so until I walked into my house where my mom and step-dad sat at the kitchen table waiting for me. They looked at me and told me to sit down at the kitchen table to talk. As I sat down, my mom started the microwave, which I assumed had a plate of food from dinner in it. My step-dad Paul slid a few pages over to me.

When I picked them up, I noticed it was the police report from the previous night. I did not care about it, but I started reading as Paul asked me for my side of the story. I filled in the parts that were not in the report or were wrong. When I finished, my mom told me that the officer who pointed a gun was arrested and released in the morning. He was being investigated which meant that someone would want to talk with me.

I was half-listening and reading until I could go to my room. When I got to the end of the report, it talked about Sara's dad getting arrested. I read that looking for some clue of where Sara went to, but I was not that lucky. When I sat the pages back on the table, my parents asked if I was OK. I didn't even consider they were asking about having a gun pointed at me.

I replied as I stood up and said "I will be, it will just take a while to accept that Sara is gone. I am going to bed; it's been a hard day for me." I turned to go up the stairs and got stopped again by Paul grabbing my arm. My mom asked me to repeat what I said. Paul was still holding my arm and asked what happened.

Reaching into my back pocket, I pulled out the note Sara left me and put it on the table next to the copy of the police report. Paul let go of my arm and was picking up the note to read. As my foot hit the first step, I stopped myself and said "Sara's dad is a bigger asshole then what most people knew. They finally got away from that drunk." I finally went upstairs to my bed. When I hit the bed, I slept and did not want to see the sun come up.

Luckily, I had friends that cared. Mark and Duke came into my room in the morning waking me up. I was hoping that it was a bad dream, even though I knew better. It was reconfirmed when Duke handed me Sara's note saying that my mom asked him to give it to me.

If it would have been any other time where my mind was in a different place, I might have fought back. But I did nothing when Duke and Mark both grabbed an arm and pulled me out of my bed. Mark reminded me that we had things to do, but the three of us could work through it. Duke pick up my pants asking if they were clean and tossed them to me before I answered.

The rest of the day, we went to Fostoria, Findlay, and would meet Mick in Fremont, then finished in Tiffin. I could not help that they kept telling me how they figured things would change. They also told me I would have to figure out how to deal with it. Mark said at least once between each stop that I should not date anyone for a while. I should look at it the way people in Alcoholics Anonymous are told to cope.

We finished the day going to a bridge out in the middle of nowhere. The bridge had a little pull off for people to go down and fish. Under the bridge was a platform with plenty of room for a small group to sit. That is where we sat and drank. Mark handed me a bottle of Makers Mark and that was the day Makers Mark became my drink of choice.

To guess the time when I was dropped back off at my house, I would say it was about ten or eleven. Walking in the house, Paul was at the table watching the evening news, and my mom I guessed was already in bed. Looking at Paul, he asked if I needed to talk. When I said no, he told me goodnight. Nothing more was said and I was finally back under my sheets.

E.A. Maynard

CHAPTER EIGHT

ABOUT A MONTH AND A half had passed since Sara had left,. The ground was covered in snow and the temperatures have dropped below freezing. Mark and Duke were right about things changing. I had become more aggressive and it was like, after every fight, my fuse got cut a little shorter.

Mark had even made comments about how I punched a few guys who owed us money. He believed that a little threatening them would have done the trick and kept better relations. He might have been right, but I was not thinking about the path of least resistance. I had anger to get out. The good thing about what I was doing was that it got people not to mess around with Mark and me.

The downside was that I built up a list of enemies. I must have had bad luck or something. One of these guys who I made an enemy with had an uncle who was pushing drugs in Fremont. I had just finished having dinner with Mick and discussed how he was growing and needed help. We made an agreement that would be the start of moving my drug business to the next level.

After dinner, Mick and I walked out and went to our cars. As I got to my car some guys grabbed me and dragged me to the back of the restaurant. There were three guys in their thirties kicking me and yelling. I was getting pissed that I had left my guns in my car. I had been carrying the .380 on my ankle but took it off because it just felt uncomfortable that day.

The guys kicking me were not doing their worst, or they did not have much strength. They stopped kicking me when they got tired or figured they had done enough. I was sore and was not moving too fast, but I didn't think anything was broken. Two of the guys walked away to a car parked by the dumpster. The third guy kneeled down and told me I made a mistake messing with his nephew Chris. I sure he thought he was scary. He added that I would get the same if he ever saw me in Fremont again.

The bastards drove away in a crappy car with more rust than should be on any car. By the time they got on the road, I was on my feet and walked to my car. I was pissed since I had mud on me, wet from some melted snow, all because I was attacked by these three guys. My anger had hit its boiling point and I would make these guys regret their life choices.

I spotted Mick sitting in his car in front of the restaurant. I caught him off guard when I knocked on his window. I noticed he was reaching for something until he realized it was me. I knew then that Mick was carrying, too. He opened his door and I heard "Bearman, what are you doing here, I thought you left? And why are you covered in mud?"

Pulling out a cigarette and a Bic lighter, I started telling him what happened, then lit my cigarette. Finally, I asked if he knew any Chris that I had beaten up recently. He made my day when he said he did. It was a guy who owes Mick money and Mick had asked me to handle it for him. Mick knew where he lived, too.

I found a payphone, called Duke and Mark and told them to get over and meet up with Mick and me. Mick suggested that we meet at the trade school Vanguard since that was close to where Chris lived. They agreed, and I asked Mick if he had any guns.

He opened his trunk and showed me a four ten shotgun and a nice looking twelve-gauge pump. He explained how he went hunting that morning but got nothing. Mick was making my day with his information and having two guns. Now all I needed was to get Chris, and I could help his friends learn a valuable lesson.

Mick told me he would meet up with me and went his way. I drove over to the trade school to wait for everyone. Mick showed up after Duke and Mark arrived. I was about to ask why he took so long, but before I said anything, he pointed to the passenger seat of his car. "Is that Chris?" Was all I said, and Mick nodded his head to say yes.

I walked over to talk to the guy and recognized him the moment I saw his face. He still had the black eye I gave him. I got into the back seat of Mick's car and had a nice chat with him. I would try it Mark's way. "Chris, you know you're in some shit, right? Before you say anything, I want to make sure you understand how deep you are. First, I have three options. It all depends on if you tell me the truth or lie to me. If you tell us the truth, you will be free to go."

If you lie to me, I will have to decide if I will shoot you so you have to crap in a bag for the rest of your life, or if I shoot you and shove my forty-five into your back and blow your chest off. Either way you want to look at it, lying will not be good for you."

Nothing more was said when Chris promised to be as honest as he could. He started to swear to God, his mother, and a few other things. I stopped him and asked who he had come after me. I thought it was a simple question, but he kept looking down and saying um. To help him along, I told him that not answering is the same as lying.

Either that did the trick for him or it could be that he heard me load a bullet into the chamber. He told me his uncle saw him with a black eye and he told his uncle what happened. Chris gave me the names and description. How it sounded, he tried to give him every detail he could about me except my birthday. Once he finished and apologized about it, I strongly encouraged him to take us to where his uncle lived.

He agreed and we both got out of Mick's car and I lead him to mine. After Chris got into my car, I told everyone what my general plan was. Mark was the only one who had an issue with it, but he agreed if I promised not to kill anyone on purpose.

I agreed and Mick got his guns, putting them in the trunk of my car. Duke and Mick climbed in the back making, Chris sit in the center. No one liked sitting there. Mark sat upfront with me and he decided to tell me how the last month was worse than working under Deatz. He reminded me that the only reason he did it was to pay bills and make sure his brother could finish school.

Most likely everyone in the back had to feel uncomfortable, but Mark and I kept discussing it. By the time we drove by Hayes Presidential Memorial Park, I had agreed to work on getting my anger back in line. Mick and Duke from the back made comments about how they were glad to hear that too. Mark said that people had started getting nervous about doing business with us.

Chris was the only one not saying anything, and had looked more scared by the time we got to where his uncle lived. Since his uncle lived on a very short road (a road in town by Hayes?) that was a dead-end, I was not going to go down it. If something went wrong, I wanted to make sure we did not get trapped. Paranoia sometimes got the best of me, but I liked the saying "It's better to be safe than sorry."

I was not sure where I was going to park until I went to turn around at the next street and noticed an empty parking lot behind a city building. The parking lot was next to some tennis courts, so I figured it would work perfectly for what I wanted. There was snow packed on the road from everyone driving on it. The night had hidden away the day. Now the only light you could see was from people's houses and the few streetlights that were working.

Looking out over an open field of grass-covered by snow as we sat in my car, Mark had to ask one last time. "Are you sure you can't let this go? We can just go and smoke some weed, then talk about why you have been holding onto so much anger."

I would have given Mark a response but I was still pissed at what those guys did and hating the world, and I needed to cause some damage. Not to mention I was a little sore from being kicked. Instead, I looked in the back and told Chris that he should stay in the car or I would deal with him again. He nodded his head and I got out of my car. Everyone else followed me, but this time, no one said a word. As we walked the few blocks down Tiffin street to Sunset Trailer Ct., Duke asked why we could not be out walking around Fremont on a warmer night.

It was cold with a lite breeze coming across our face. It was only about a five minutes' walk and for Chris's uncle, he should have been happy about that. I was not going to change my plan, but the walk did help me clear my mind.

When we got to the trailer that Chris's Uncle was living in, I pulled out the Smith & Weston forty-five I was given. Spinning the cylinder, I looked at my friends and they either gave me a thumbs up or a nod. Knowing that they were with me and ready, I kicked in that thin door. The moment the door lock broke away making a cracking sound, it swung open and made a thud as it hit something. Everything felt as it was going in slow motion. It was an odd feeling to experience.

When my foot landed, the guys inside screamed and two of them dropped to the ground. I entered the mobile home that this guy lived in and it looked like shit. The carpet was a dark brown and a decade past needing changed, but the walls were even worse. They were covered in yellow tar from all the smoking done in there. There were a few spots that the original off-white color shown.

The furniture put me in mind of what would be found on the side of the road for the trash guys to get. Then I noticed the three guys. This was the first time I got a good look at them. They looked like they belonged in this crap container one of them called a home. I could not help but think that I could have kicked these guys asses if I was not caught off guard. The guy still sitting in a chair started to scream. The two on the ground must have thought I was the police. They had their hands on their head and were laying on their stomachs.

Mick followed me in, then Duke followed him. Mark came in last but barely got past the doorway. I went to the guy screaming and hit him with the side of my gun. He shut up after that and now all three were on the ground. Nudging my head towards the other rooms got Duke to walk around and see if there was anyone else was in the mobile home.

I was dealing with a lot at first. Earlier I got jumped and was somewhat beaten for the first time from someone other than Cameron. I had been asked not to kill anyone for the first time. As I stood looking at the guys laying on the floor, I was identifying people by their shoes for the first time. These guys were the ones I wanted, so it appeared that Chris would get to walk away untouched.

Two of the guys wore old tennis shoes that were close to falling apart. These were the same two guys who kicked me. The other guy had a pair of work boots that were not new, but clean. He was not the type to have seen a day of work in his life.

If any of these guys tried something, Mark would be the last to act. That is why I had him blindfold the two guys wearing tennis shoes and take them outside. While Mark was doing that, Duke came back with a dog. The thing was small and was licking him like it had not had any attention. Duke found its leash and seeing Mark trying to direct two blindfolded guys out, he helped.

Mick oddly enough had become my friend in a way, but it was more like a friend from work. You like hanging out with them, but you know that it ends after one of you finds a new job. Then again, he was the one next to me saying that he didn't promise not to shoot anyone. I don't think Mick would have shot to kill if I asked him to, but it was good to hear. I thanked him and the guy on the floor started to whimper, then asked God to help him.

This bastard was about to learn the lesson I was always

told before being kicked out of church. God only helps those who help themselves. He had helped himself into this mess, I was left to judge his fate. I knelt and rested my gun on the side of his face. It made me feel good that he was the one who I hit with it before. He already knew the cold metal feeling, so it was a reminder as it moved the gun up to his face and routed the revolver's cylinder.

"I think you know who I am, if not, I'm Scott Bearman. Remember, the guy you jumped and warned me to stay out of Fremont. I will give you a better offer. You have one month to get out of Northwest Ohio. Since you don't have anything worth packing or selling, it should be easy. If I see you again, I will put you in the hospital and to top it off, I will use this gun to make you a eunuch. Do you understand the generosity I am giving you?"

After I stopped talking for a few moments, Chris's uncle told me he understood. Well, almost everything. He said he was confused by me saying he has nothing to sell or pack. With a smile, I lit up a cigarette and told him that I always felt bad to hear how someone lost everything in a fire. That got him to lift his head enough to look at me. Before he had a chance to say anything, I gave him some extra advice. "Think how quickly we found you. Now think how quickly we will find all your family if anyone finds out any of my friends or myself were here. You left a cigarette on the counter and a fire started."

Mick looked at me like what the hell while I stood up and kicked the guy in the soft part of his side. He groaned and I looked around at the crap everywhere. Finally, I found some papers next to a window with curtains and I knew how to do it. I asked Mick to pick him up and informed him we all were about to leave. Chris's uncle and Mick both looked concerned. I think Mick was more confused while the uncle was finally realizing why I said he had nothing to pack or sell.

It was not hard to figure it out as I crumbled paper and put it in a pile. Then I took some clothes that were thrown around and put them closer to the paper. The thing I liked best was when I sat a bottle of rubbing alcohol next to everything and knocked it over. The flames took off as I used my lighter to get it going. Amazing how fast it moved in that small mobile home.

The wall was on fire and spreading to the ceiling by the time it took me to take four steps to stand next to Mick. Mick was edging to the door as the flames moved toward us. The amount of smoke was something I didn't expect. It was getting too much and I didn't have to say anything as Mick got out while dragging Chris's uncle with him. I followed as I tossed my cigarette towards the fire.

When we got to where everyone else was, Duke and Mark stood there with their mouths open. Mark asked what happened and Duke asked if the smoke from the fire was bad for us. Mick had let Chris's uncle go and he fell to the wet ground and I watched his face. Everyone but the blindfolded guys were asking what was happening. It was the first time I saw someone filled with as much anger as I felt, but he and I both knew he couldn't do anything about it. I had destroyed someone and made him live with it. It was like my anger had been passed along.

It was over and now I could move on. I also needed to get moving before the police and fire departments showed up. I knelt down one last time next to the poor guy watching his home go up in flames, then reminded him of my promise if anyone heard we were there. Pure rage could be heard in his voice as he agreed and told me he will be leaving Ohio. Giving a signal, Mark, Duke, and Mick started to walk away. I removed the guys blindfolds. Pointing to the fire I reminded them if they say anything about me or my friends, that their homes would be next.

Neither of them said a thing, so I hoped they understood. I was off and at a good speed, jogged to catch up with everyone. Duke looked back and when I got up to them, he said I had a big glow behind me. Oddly enough, we all made jokes and had a good walk kicking snow at each other. All four of us walked back down the road to my car, side by side and as Duke said, "we had a glow."

To my surprise, Chris was still sitting in the car. He stared in the direction of his uncle's place as we climbed into the car. Not a word was spoken on the drive back to the trade school's parking lot. When we got there, Chris finally asked what happened. I could see he wanted to ask on the drive back. Every time I looked in the mirror, he would make a face as if he were about to say something. Mark surprised me by saying that his uncle would be relocating. He told Chris that he would be smart to remember he was somewhere else the whole time. We all got out and Chris was off to I don't know where. It was the last time I ever saw him.

The guns got put back in Mick's car and we all said our goodbyes. Duke and Mick took off first, leaving Mark and me to talk. Mark and I sat inside my car talking with the heater going. Mark told me that he was going to back out of what we have created. He told me how he felt that I had built everything and had him along for the ride. He only asked if I would give up a few guys so he could keep money coming. It never dawned on me that he felt that way, or when he said that, he perhaps felt I would get too big and find a world of problems.

We didn't say anything for a bit. We smoked our cigarettes until they were finished. Mark got out of the car, but before closing the door said that he still wanted to hang out. I liked that and let him know I would see when we all can get together.

He closed the door and he was off. I was back to being by myself, which was a common thing with all the driving I did. This time, I had a clear head for the first time since Sara left. Driving back to Risingsun allowed me to think about how much I missed Sara, but really, I hoped she was safe and happy.

E.A. Maynard

CHAPTER NINE

MARK WENT ON TO DO his own thing. It had been maybe two or three weeks, and I had been too busy dealing with everything to think about what had happened. My meet–ups with the guys I had networked with was stretching me thin. I only had time to find the fastest route to the next place. I even missed a week of school to make my deals. That bothered me a lot too. I refused to be a dropout or fail. I wouldn't be one of those people not thinking about the future. I was taught to expect everything will end someday.

It was while waiting for a guy passing through from New York to Chicago that I had time to think. I was questioning that Deatz would keep his side by teaching me everything I needed to know. I set up a business under my name a few days ago and Deatz was little help. In fact, Deatz was distancing himself from me. He was keeping the pricing we agreed on, but everything else was a challenge to get out of him.

Mick and I had been working together more, but only in Fremont. It was funny how in four months my business had grown. I had given up three guys to Mark who were not a lot of work to deal with. They could make a couple hundred a month for him if he kept up with them. That should pay his bills and maybe put some back. Either way, he seemed to be happy from when we hung out a few days ago.

I didn't hold a grudge against Mark since I knew he was not trying to hurt me by stepping away. He wanted to get away from anything that had to do with drugs, but he had to take care of his brother. I can respect that; people should take care of family if they can. I was well aware that not everyone had a life as good as I did. I was working on building my small business to make money and become more powerful. The problem I was learning about when getting more power was how others want to take it away or keep what the power they have.

I believed Deatz was one of these people who felt I was taking it from him. His behavior towards me was not helping since Mark and I split our business. Plus, Mark made a comment that Deatz was trying to ramp up things with the guy from Chicago but did not want me to know. I might have been being paranoid, but it felt as Deatz was cutting me out of a lot of things we had been working on.

I am not sure if Deatz had ever hurt anyone, at least not more than a small beating or breaking a bone. I did fear that he might consider eliminating me to take over the business I had built. If he got me out of the way, my little enterprise could be his. It did not cross my mind on how much I told Deatz about what I was doing. I even told him about how I kept a notebook to track who needed what and an address book of who I dealt with.

It was not the best thing to think about while waiting for the supplier. When the supplier finally showed up, we talked since he wanted to stretch his legs. Plus, I think he was happy to talk with someone. That is when I asked if they had a guy selling out of Chicago. Clearly, that was not the right thing to ask considering the look on his face.

"What do you mean? Did someone from Chicago talk to you? If they did, we will take care of them." He thought for a moment while looking at me in the eyes. It was a creepy feeling to have this guy not breaking eye contact while standing there. I don't know what was going over in his head. Then he asked me if I knew why Deatz's orders went down. He explained that there was talk about how my sales doubled everything that Deatz had sold. Then

Deatz's orders went back down.

We had changed our procedure and only my product was coming from the guys out of New York City. The delivery guy must have figured I looked concerned or something. He told me to relax and told me about how John rewarded people with information. It turned out that the reward went further up the ladder the more John felt he was betrayed. All I had to do was get all the details and call a number to have John call me back.

Two things scared me about doing this. The first was I would be going against Deatz. If he found out, he probably would kill me and not in a quick way. The second was John, and how he would take my information. I had heard stories about what John has done to people. If he thought I was part of what Deatz was doing and covering my ass, then would I be killed too, at least that was my concern.

The delivery guy told me about a guy in Pittsburgh who betrayed John. From the description of what happened, he suffered. Then he had his driver's license stuck on him so the guy could be identified. The thought of it made me shiver. The driver took off after that, and I was off to meet Mick.

I had become more relaxed with having drugs in my car by this time. While Mick and I ate at another greasy spoon restaurant, I was not concerned about what was in my trunk. I even parked next to a cop car. It took the waitress some time to get our order.

While we waited, I noticed the cops sitting with a guy who pointed a gun at me. He sat there with three other guys. Two were in uniform and the third was in regular clothes, but I would have guessed him to be a cop, too.

The two cops left shortly after I noticed them. A plan dawned on me at that moment and I put it into action when the third guy went to the restroom. Walking over to his table, our eyes met and he was pissed to see me. That was OK, since he would be in a better mood after we talked. Mick sat at the table watching me as I sat down across from the state trooper.

"I will make this quick. I might have a bad memory or remember something in your favor at the trial coming up for you. I need you to work with me on some things. It won't be that bad and you will look good afterward. That is not all; I can give you a little cash to help." After I finished and waited for him to respond, he gave me the come-on waving jester.

I explained that I knew of some people pushing lots of drugs. I added how knowing about some people that need a warning if anyone is coming for them would be helpful for me.

He made sure he was clear when he told me he was interested. We were about to make a deal, but his friend came back. He stood there looking down at me sitting in his chair as if I was supposed to be scared of him. If he only knew the people I dealt with. I decided not to play hard ass with the guy and give him his seat back. I started getting up until the guy put his hand on my shoulder and sat in another chair.

It is not always a good idea to talk about blackmail and bribery in front of random people, but I took a chance to see what played out. In front of both of them, I offered two hundred dollars to each of them for protection. I promised we would be supplying information on competitors so they could look good. There would also be an extra hundred for helping me or any of my guys to keep us out of trouble. If they needed help, we could figure out how to be good friends. The guy who I had never seen before asked why I was making him the offer.

In the nicest voice, I told him that it would be rude to make an offer to one cop and not the other at the table. That got me a look of contempt from my soon to be new friend. When I explained why I knew he was a cop, he boldly asked for five hundred a month.

Even though I could afford that much, I wanted to make sure they knew turning on me would be bad. To make it easier for them to understand, I told the new guy I was the minor his buddy had just pointed a gun at. I was also scheduled to give my account in a hearing.

With the last bit of confidence I had, I stood up and pointed to Mick and said "I am going to eat my food and if I leave without an answer, I will take your silence as a no. If that is the case, best of luck in your next job." Without drama, I turned and went back to my table and Mick.

Mick started asking what the hell I just did. He was trying to act calm, but I knew him enough to know he was barely holding it together. I had just made a move I never thought I would do. I had blackmailed a cop and offered bribes to two cops. All in a matter of minutes and the whole time pretending it was a normal thing for me. I told Mick everything I said and how I was secretly freaking out.

That got him to laugh loud enough that a few people looked in our direction. Even the two cops looked at us, as well. Mick is the one who saw them looking and told me they did not look happy. It was when we stopped laughing, I felt a hand on my shoulder. Without thinking I reached for my .380. Luckily Mick put his hand up as if he knew what I was doing. Of course, it was the same cop that had pointed a gun at me before.

Both cops sat down with Mick and me. Mick, being a smart ass, looked at them and said "Sooo, which one of you likes to pull his gun on teenagers? Not that I am judging, just want to know who not to piss off." Mick's comment allowed me to learn something new about him because of what the new cop said.

"You know you look like your dad. It's hard to miss. I always wondered if he is as big of a bastard when he is not wearing the badge. So?"

Mick told him that his dad is a bastard no matter what. After that, no one was looking happy, but I did not care if they were happy. I only wanted to hear them agree to what I had proposed to them. I knew that my stunt could backfire on me, but if they went with my offer, I would have something Deatz did not, which was having cops working for me. That could be very helpful if Deatz turned on me.

It made my day when the cop I meant to blackmail leaned in and said they wanted a grand each. That told me that I had them on the hook. We went back and forth for about five minutes when we made an agreement. I would give them a hundred-dollar bonus when they arrested a competitor, and they had to keep them off the streets for more than a week. Plus another three hundred bonus when they helped get someone out of trouble who worked with me. They both gave me their information and walked out thinking they got the best of me.

Mick told me how surprised he was about how it went and how we now have two cops in our pockets. He kept talking about how we could do more and what he thought we could do. It was good to hear him keep saying we. I decided to ask Mick if he would like to help me handle my guys. In return, I promised to give him a small cut of my profits. After we worked out the deal for what he would do for me, Mick threw out a thought of how we could expand on what he had agreed to do.

I liked what he proposed, and it could make my life easier. Instead of me trying to build up a group of people in each town, Mick suggested we put a person in charge of the towns or designated areas. We could help them build up the people under them. This meant I would not have to meet up with several guys in a town. Instead, I could set up regular meetings and work my schedule better. He would also handle some of the guys around him and expand farther past Fremont.

Between working with Mick more and putting his plan into effect, I could get back to finishing school. Plus my stress level should go down. It was clear that making Mick the offer and having him replace Mark was a good idea. He just would not be a fifty-

fifty partner.

What started out feeling as a bad day had turned into something very good. On that note, I said goodbye to Mick and went to meet up with Deatz. Even though the drugs I had was all for me, I still had to let him see it and give him the cash I owed him. It was not hard for me to think about how much better business would be without him. I am not sure if I got a chill from thinking about how to get rid of Deatz or if it was the breeze from the holes in my floorboard.

The breeze broke my thoughts and I decided I needed to bite the bullet to get a new car. The rest of the drive to Fostoria was thinking about what I wanted. First, I thought about a Jeep and the fun I would have with the top down. It even made me smile to think about having a pretty girl next to me while the wind blew through our hair. Sadly though, I decided that I needed something practical that would help me get work done. I decided on getting a nice pickup truck. I could haul large orders, and no one would look too close to a pickup.

It was not long after I made my decision that I was at Deatz's place. I had no urge to rush in and deal with him. The alternative was to sit in my car and waste gas. Plus, I drove out of my way to get to his place and drop off the drugs. I did not know why I needed to even bring the drugs in since it was all mine. It would make sense to give Deatz the cash and deal with everything myself. With that thought, I headed in to make the delivery and discuss some changes to what we were doing.

He had to have watched me come up. The moment I stepped onto the porch, the door opened and Deatz made a smart-ass comment. He was acting smug and I could only think about how it would be easy to get rid of him with a call to John. His only saving grace was how scared I was of John and if he thought I was misleading him. Deatz did make it easy to imagine how enjoyable making that call would be.

I dropped the duffel in the living room and as I started to talk to Deatz, another guy walked in. The guy looked like the guy I saw that time Deatz and Mark took a trip to Chicago. This time, I found out who he was. Turns out that he was Deatz's cousin and an ass, too. I would have never guessed they were cousins. Deatz was a tall dark black guy that was a bit overweight, but you could see he had muscles hidden under the juglines. His cousin had a lighter complexion as if he was mixed and matched my height. The other difference was Deatz's cousin looked at me as if he feared me.

I sat down waiting for them to finish talking. As far as I was concerned, if it did not affect me, I did not care. That is why it did not bother me when the cousin asked Deatz for a few hundred-dollar loan. Deatz asked if I would go check on the dogs in the back yard. Once I was out of the room, they started to talk again but talked at a normal level. So, I could hear Deatz ask why he needs another loan as I made my way through his kitchen and to the back yard.

I was only out with the dogs for five minutes when Deatz knocked on the door to let me know to come in so we could do our thing. Entering the house again, I noticed that Deatz looked stressed this time. Good thing for me, I did not care if I put more stress on him. He sat at his kitchen table and asked why I was not to his house sooner. There was no way I was going to tell him about how I got two cops in my pocket. I did tell him that I got a bite to eat with one of my guys and discussed how to improve things. That caught Deatz's attention, but I blew past it and started in with my plan to stop coming by with the drugs. It took some time for Deatz to get on board. Once he was, we had agreed that I would bring him his money when I dropped off my request for the following order.

Since I did not have anything more to discuss, I walked to the living room and grabbed the bags. My goal at that moment was simple, get out, sort everything, and go home for some sleep. Unfortunately, that is not what happened. Deatz followed me into the living room and as I lifted the bags, he asked me about my family. Before I got to answer, he asked what I thought about his cousin. I wanted to ask how the hell would I know anything to be able to judge him. Instead, I told Deatz that some family members are a pain, but it's not like you can strangle them to death. Then I joked about how I tried that once with one of my cousins. Everyone got upset about it. Deatz looked at me and asked if that was me being a smart ass or if it really happened. He understood when I said that I let go of him when he passed out and for a guy twice my weight, he went down quite easily.

That got a laugh out of him. He went on to tell me about how his cousin can't seem to hold onto a job and comes to Deatz asking for a loan with no payback date. Deatz had given him a loan a few times, but it had become a nuisance. It came across as funny to me that he was coming to me about his family issues.

After twenty minutes of listening to Deatz talk, I made him an offer. I would talk to his cousin and see if he would be able to work for a guy I knew. Deatz agreed and I took that as my opening to leave.

Bags in hand again and about to open the door when Deatz said one last thing. "I know you're trying to cut me out of your business, and I don't care. But you need to remember that you will always have to go through me. If you try to go around me, no one will find your body. I am not easy to take down like your cousin was in your story. Now get out of here and make me some money."

I didn't reply to him. I imagined that Deatz was planning something to make sure I was stuck under him. If not, why would he throw that in? I figured that would be something to think about on the road. I got out and went to Mark's house since it was close, and I could talk to Mark while sorting. Plus, Mark could help me get everything done. It wouldn't be his first time.

E.A. Maynard

CHAPTER TEN

MARK WAS HOME AND HE was happy to talk with me while I did my sorting. It might sound bad, but I was happy that his mom was passed out again. Last time I showed up, she would not leave me alone till I gave her something to "Dull the pain and dreams" as she said. I had known people that lost a loved one, but none took it as hard as she acted.

It was a strange feeling doing my business stuff with Mark, as we were no longer partners. Mark didn't seem to care, but then he was the one who left. He only wanted to do enough to get through until Jay finished school. Once I got past the odd feeling, it was like old times.

We talked and joked around till I finished. Mark didn't help, but that was OK with me. I had a warm place to do my work and a friendly conversation. Plus, I had a good laugh when I was leaving, as Jay tried to tell me he could triple my income if I made him my partner. That boy could not improve anything unless it was his chance to end up dead or in prison.

It dawned on me that Jay would most likely become a dealer, too. That kid was going to do everything wrong and have no clue it was all his own doing. At least I was aware that I might go to jail, but it will be because of my choices. The problem I see when it comes to Jay, Mark would blame himself.

Driving down the road, I could not help wondering what would be the mistake that would send me to prison. It would not be for selling to an undercover cop. With Mick's idea, I would only be selling to those that I already knew. The only logical thing I could think of would be that everyone turned on each other. One person gets arrested and everyone else would follow. One telling on another and so on. All I could think was oh crap, I am going to prison because someone will do something stupid.

The thought got so bad, I pulled over to the side of the road. I sat there for about ten minutes when an older guy stopped to check on me. It was nice of him, but considering I had several thousand dollars' worth of drugs in my trunk, I got a little nervous. I saw the headlights pull up behind me and could only see a cop stopping. I don't think I took a breath the whole time it took him to walk up to my car. I exhaled a big breath of relief when I saw he was not a cop.

The guy knocked on my passenger door and I rolled down my window. Considering I had my .380 loaded and in an easy to reach place, I was not too concerned if this guy tried something. He was a tall guy that looked like he worked hard for a living and had a hard life. I had never seen him before, but we talked in general terms and as strange as it sounds, he gave me some advice that stuck with me.

"We all have problems; some are very bad and some we just think are bad. Either way, there are two places to look. I always find my answers in the Bible or watching the Godfather." After that, the stranger wished me luck, asked if I needed any help, and got back on his way. I thought about it and I didn't think the good book was going to tell me how to keep people from talking. I would go find a copy of the Godfather tomorrow after my deliveries were finished.

I made Mick my first stop since he was an early riser and I wanted to hear if he had any more thoughts about my business. To my surprise, he had already started a map of our area broken into regions or territories. Looking at it, I instantly knew who I could use for what areas. What made it easier was how we could make all the deliveries in a single day. It would be nice to do all the deliveries and still have time left in the day. He had a route drawn showing where we could do a drop and go on our way.

I was excited and wished it was already that way, but two things needed to be done. First, I had to find out if the guys I had in mind would be interested in doing the job. The other thing I needed to do was make sure they would be able to do the work.

I can't figure out how I had gotten into a real business. I only wanted to make money and have fun. Either way, whatever I had made, I needed to get everything in order.

I got lucky and spoke with three of the seven guys I wanted to talk with and even found a copy of all three of The Godfather movies. I didn't realize that there were three of these movies. I only hoped that they were good movies.

It took me another three days until I spoke with everyone. I got six of the seven onboard and excited about what we could do.

The day after getting the six guys agreeing to join me, I finally had time to sit down and watch the movie. My family joined me and we made a night of it. We ate popcorn with butter and garlic salt, as we sat with the lights dimmed. After the movie was done, I could only ask why we had never watched it before. Paul and my mom made fun of me, but told me that the first is the best of the three Godfather movies.

There was no arguing that the stranger who talked with me on the side of the road was right when he said the best answers are found in one of two places. The movie had shown me how to make sure no one turned on me. The guys and I needed to be a family. I had helped a few of the guys, so I had built my trust and reputation to the point that others believed in me.

That was a foundation I could work with. I only needed to make sure none of them would be like Fredo. Fredo was the older brother to the Godfather and went against his family.

In my mind, I ran different ways to do this, until I realized that family always takes care of its own. I had gotten blood on my hands while working out my rage over losing Sara. In doing that, I had people both fear me and respect me. I needed the guys who would be working with me to have the same thing. I did not know if it would work, but I would do my best to have my name be enough for them to use as a tool.

By being the protective brother to them, I hoped would build the family type of connection I was going for. I thought about it in great detail to know that I wanted to be looked at as the head, but also an equal when having discussions and trust. Brothers have a simple rule. They can say what they want about their brother, but if someone else does it, then a good old fight might follow. That is what I wanted.

After putting my plan together, I would have my name feared even more. I only needed to figure out who to use so that it worked. I called Mark and Duke to see if they wanted to meet up. Out of everyone I knew, they could tell people a rumor and no one would question them. Mark had gotten the word around about the Dan guy and made sure everyone knew I did what I did for a good reason. Duke was a trustworthy person. I watched Duke meet someone and was friends before he finished a cigarette.

They both agreed to meet up. Now I needed to get them to get on board with me. They would be the key in making my plan work. I would not trust anyone else with pulling this off. We went to a girl's house in Fostoria who was seeing Mark. I think Mark wanted us to meet this girl. He made a comment about her when I was over at his place sorting.

It was a nice house and the girl seemed very nice. She was a dirty blonde that was a bit short, but a beautiful girl. We hit it off and had a good time and most of the time, we didn't get a chance to talk about what I wanted to. Mark's girl was named Stacey and Stacey fit into the group as if she had been part of the group for some time.

The one thing Stacey didn't do was smoke, so when I went out to have a cigarette, the other guys came with me.

That is when we discussed my plan. I explained how I wanted to have the Bearman name hold fear for anyone considering doing something against me. I gave them three rumors that I hoped would do the trick. Mark suggested another one and they talked between each other figuring what to say. It made me happy to have friends that would not ask why or what they got out of helping me. Instead, we smoked and discussed what the rumors should be. We ended up smoking two cigarette while working out the details.

The rest of the evening was Stacey asking Duke about Jenny, and telling me about a girl named Carri. It was nice that she was trying to connect with Duke and me, but I didn't have any interest in seeing anyone. I zoned off for a bit, all the while they talked about things that didn't involve me. Then Mark bumped me to bring me back to from my thoughts.

In a sweet voice I heard "Bearman, are you going to come next Friday? It wouldn't be as fun without you." Stacey had planned with Duke that we all would go to Jenny's house since Jenny's parents would be out of town. That meant drinking and all sorts of crazy memories. That thought got me to agree, plus we tend to always have a good time. I don't know why Stacey got excited about me agreeing, but she came over and hugged me.

I had a feeling that there might be more to it, but I would not worry about it for now. We finished the evening with Duke and me heading to his house. Mark stayed with his girlfriend for a while after we were gone. Who could blame him, a beautiful girl really does make things seem nicer. When we got to Duke's house, Duke told me that I should have paid attention. Mark's new girlfriend said that she would invite Carri for me to meet.

I could have kicked myself, but that would be a concern for another day. My worries still were focused on Deatz and trying to figure out what he was planning to do. I did not say anything to Mark because I did not want him to say anything to Deatz. I told Duke so I could get his feedback. If I am going to cross someone like Deatz, I wanted a second option.

I told Duke about what happened with the delivery guy. I explained how he wanted me to get information on Deatz buying from some guy in Chicago. Telling Duke about my fear of Deatz learning that I betrayed him and what he would do, Duke thought about it awhile. He sat there in a chair making a few noises. It was very annoying to listening to him.

Finally, he answered me and in his own fashion, he acted as if he had come up with an answer for a universal question. He said "The world you're in is not a safe one. You knew that when you started. The question is, how far do you want to go?" Then he leaned back into his chair and stared at me.

He could have said it without the cockiness. I knew he was right, and I did not get into selling drugs because it was safe. Now that I had built up a network with Mick's help, I would be making it bigger and stronger. The only answer I could come up with would be to make the call to John. I only needed to get more information before I made the call.

That is what I did, too. With the help of Mick and a few other guys, I got enough to call John when I was ready. I would hold off from calling John immediately. With everything I learned, Deatz had been planning on this for a while. As smart as I thought he was, in two weeks, I found out that he had bragged about his business to several people.

Then I took the time to talk to Deatz's cousin. I talked with him about me helping him get a job an illegal casino. The key to working for that kind of place is to be able to keep your mouth shut. Deatz's cousin had a problem with that. He only had a beer and a joint before he told me about how he was going to Chicago with Deatz. I knew everything that was planned for the next month. By the time I left, I knew two things. The first would be this guy would be killed after a week if I got him the job at the casino. The second would be that I had a few weeks to use this against Deatz.

After I finished getting every detail I needed, I told him I would mention him to the illegal casino. He would not be happy if they took him in. Either way, I will keep my promise and let Deatz deal with the outcome. I also considered that Deatz was close to his cousin and would not take it well if something happened to him. It might even have him do something stupid. Deatz was tough as the next guy with a one on one challenge, but he would not do good going to fight a group by himself.

I could enjoy doing this. Putting Deatz on guard with two fronts would make him fall so much easier. If he is smart, he would run and hide from the people he had pissed off. I honestly don't know if he was that smart. If he chose to stay and let his pride get the best of him, he would be responsible for his own actions. I would only help things move along and work on taking any power from him that I could.

I let another week pass when I decided to make the call to John. I did not know how much it would cost to make a call from Ohio to New York City, which is why I ended up with ten dollars' worth of quarters. We can say it was overkill, but I did not want to lose the call because I did not plan well enough. I was only on the call for a few seconds and left a message with some lady who told me to stay by the payphone for up to an hour for a return call.

I don't know how long I waited when the phone rang. I know I smoked three cigarettes and drank half a bottle of soda. The ringing of that payphone made me jump and fumbling to get to the phone. I was about to turn Deatz in and I had no idea what I truly was getting myself into. When I did answer the phone, the guy on the other line told me that I needed to be quick and tell them everything I knew. Since I was dealing with real mobsters, I was not going to act like a hard ass. I made sure I was clear in telling him everything I had learned.

Finishing my report with "Will this get back to John?" led to an answer I did not expect. The guy on the phone told me that he was John. That led him to tell me what would be happening after we hung up. John was clearly not happy as I could hear it in his voice. I could almost hear a smile when he said he would be bringing my delivery of supplies in two weeks. I had to figure out a nice steak house for us to have dinner after he had met with Deatz. The phone went dead after that and I stood there holding the phone.

What would I do? I figured I would deal with one of John's guys as I had done before. I had a few things to do, so I hung the phone up and got on my way. I almost forgot about the get together at Jenny's house and a meet up in Pemberville, Ohio. I made it to my meeting with the guy who was covering the farm towns around Pemberville. It was nice that Pemberville was not a far drive from Jenny's place in Gibsonburg.

CHAPTER ELEVEN

PULLING UP TO JENNY's house, I was the last person there. Duke and Mark were parked in front of the house and didn't leave me a spot to park. The only place left to part was in front of a house across the street. I had noticed from before that an older couple lived in the house.

Not to be rude since it was a small town, I knocked on the front door. I learned years ago that an upset neighbor could cause several headaches. It was only a few moments after I knocked when the old guy opened the door. He looked as though I upset him with just knocking and was about to lay into me. In a stern voice, he asked me what I wanted and told me to be quick about it.

As I explained my parking issue and asked for permission to park in front of his house, his wife yelled from inside the house. I could not help but laugh at what she said. "Hector, when you're done playing hard-ass, how about you invite the boy in so I can hear him too." She said that in such a matter of fact way that Hector just smiled and told me to come in.

If it was not for all the pictures all over of their house of family, I would not have known they were grandparents. Hector was a tall dark and OK looking guy who I figured like to mess with people when he could. His wife came in with two glasses of water and asked me to sit down at the table with them. She told me to call her Milli, then I gave my name to them.

They both got a look on their face that reminded me of eating something very sour. Hector in a firm voice and a straight

97

face asked who my family was. I could have lied to make this go easier, but I didn't see the point in it. I told them my father is Cameron Bearman from Gibsonburg. I told them that means I am related to the rest of the Bearman's in town.

Milli told me that she thought the world of my grandpa. As for the rest of the Bearman family, she said they belonged in the city dump with the rest of the trash. Hector laughed about that and told me she was trying to be nice since I belonged to them. That is when I quickly corrected him. "Sir, I am not a saint, but I am not part of them. I only share their last name. They made that clear to me when I was ten and have reminded me of that fact ever since. I am glad too, as my family is from Risingsun and we are a working bunch. We earn our money and only fight to protect family or friends."

Both Milli and Hector told me that they were happy to hear that. We had a nice chat after that and I came to really like them. They had given me permission to park there whenever I needed. As I was leaving, I told them I would be across the street and doing un-saintly things. Then I asked them to let me know if we bother them, and if we do, I would quiet everyone down. They told me to have fun, but not to be too crazy.

The door shut behind me and I walked over to Jenny's where Duke and Mark were out front smoking. When they noticed me, they walked to meet me. I don't know why, because they only got off the porch when we were together. They joked about me leaving the old people's house. That was till I said it is better to be on good terms with the neighbors and not have the cops called while we are drinking.

I had lit my cigarette up when the girls come out to join us. Jenny and Stacey, I already knew, but there was a third girl who I had to guess was Carri. She was a cute girl with dyed black hair and wearing a pair of baggy grunge bell-bottom pants. Her pants hid the shoes with very thick soles. Those shoes made her as tall as I was and taller than the other girls.

Her first interaction with me was to walk up and take my cigarette from me. She looked me dead square in the eyes while taking a drag of it. I was not sure if she was trying to be cute or seem like a tough girl, but I was not impressed with her little trick. I was hoping that she was going to show me more than her trying to be a bad girl.

Don't get me wrong, a bad girl can be fun to spend time with. It does lose its entertainment value after a bit. Since Sara had vanished, I had been set up on six dates. Two of them tried acting like bad girls. One of them got nervous when a guy I used to sell to, came over after our dinner and asked for a dime bag. I nicely told the guy who to go see for what he wanted. Let's say that scared her off in a hurry.

Carri did not come across as an act, but rather someone that had to show she was tough to get through life. Stacey and Jenny went back to the house to warm up, leaving Carri and us guys to smoke while talking. I understood Carri more as she talked. She told me about walking over to the bowling alley from the apartment that her and her mom lived in. The only apartments in Fostoria across from a bowling alley I knew of had some rough people in there.

I don't know how true it was, but a buddy working at the local Pizza Hut told me that they stopped delivering there. He said it was because the drivers kept getting robbed.

I listened to her talk and thinking about those apartments, while Duke and Mark went inside. It was not bitter cold out, but it was still far from a summer day. I put my coat on her to help keep her warm, but she tried to hand it back.

I stopped her and told her that I had almost a hundred pounds on her and two shirts on, I would be fine. After we got everything out of the way, it was nice talking with her. Carri never knew her dad and didn't care if she ever did. My father was garbage to use Milli's phrasing. I was about to suggest we go in when I heard Hector yelling my name.

Carri went inside Jenny's house while I went to see if there was anything I could do for Hector. Come to find out, he was helping me out. He handed me two bottles of wine, then asked if anyone was driving for the night. When I promised we all would be staying in, he told me to be good and went back to his house. Walking into Jenny's house, I told her how much I liked her neighbor. Even though she grew up across the street from them, she never talked to them. She told me how that was going to change.

Mark opened his book bag and pulled out three bottles of Mad Dog 20/20, a bottle of Jack Daniels, and a bottle of Makers Mark for me. That is what I call a good friend. The girls went off to find a corkscrew and Carri grabbed a bottle of 20/20 while following them. Duke grabbed the small bottle of Jack. I, of course, reached for the Makers Mark. When my hand grasped it, Mark said "You know that is our bottle? I am not that nice to you." It made me chuckle for a moment and I jokingly told him I am not afraid to share with him.

The sun had set and lots of drinking had been done. Out on the porch, as we went out for another cigarette, Carri caught us off guard with a dare. At this point, we had plenty to drink, so you knew it would not be a PG rated dare. Carri and I had been flirting and giving each other a hard time all night, too. So, when she dared us guys to run four blocks in nothing but our socks and shoes, I was the only taker.

Mark ran in and got the other two girls while Carri and I made the dare into a bet, with terms. As Stacey and Jenny came out to join us, I repeated the terms while I took off my clothes. "I have to run four blocks and do ten jumping jacks. Once I am done, I come back and you owe me a striptease."

Stacey said Carri's name in a surprised voice, but Carri

agreed. This would have been an easy bet to win on most any other night. This night I did not have lady luck running with me. My buddies stood there laughing as I put my shoes back on and two of the three girls acted like they were not looking at me.

It all went smoothly till I got to my seventh jumping jack. That is when the town cop came around the corner and their headlights hit my bare ass. I was going to turn around to see who it was till the cops turned on the flashing red and blues.

There was nothing more I needed to know. I took off running and not back to the house. I was happy that we did not have any snow on the ground. Considering this was not the first time I had to run from the Gibsonburg police, I knew a few tricks that might help my getaway. If there was snow on the ground, they might see my footsteps. Instead, when I ran down an alley they had to slow down to make the turn. As they got in the alley and turned on their spotlight, I had started running through people's backyards.

I was doing good and thought I would be in the clear when I watched the cops drive by. My outlook changed when I heard one of them get out and say he would search on foot. I had two things run through my head at that moment. First was oh crap, where can I go. The second thought was what kind of man puts so much effort into chasing a naked teenager!

I took a gamble and hid under a Dodge Dakota pickup truck. It was high enough that I could slide under and low enough you would need to bend down to look under it. That night I learned a valuable lesson. No amount of adrenaline pumping through your body can prepare you for how cold a concrete driveway feels. It might not have been so bad if it was my naked backside that was pressed against the concrete during the winter.

It must have been five minutes when I climbed back out, but every minute felt much longer than time should have felt. I started on my way and saw the cop car a few blocks away from me, but did not see or hear the guy on foot. There was nothing going to stop me from running as fast as I could and when a voice yelled: "Hey, stop," that whole adrenaline thing kicked in. I don't think I had ever run that fast in my life before or since. The sounds of his shoes clomping on the road helped drive me to push myself harder. I had to be making some distance on him from the sounds he made. There would be no looking back till I got to the alley behind Jenny's house. Her place had a tall wooden fence with a door on the backside. I just hoped it was not locked. When there was no sign of the cop, I ran to the fence door and got into her backyard. At the moment the door was closed and I was safe, every muscle in my body felt as if it would give out. I was in good shape, but I was nowhere close to being in the kind of shape it would take to do all that running in the cold and still be fine.

When I walked up to the back door a floodlight came on and I had another crappy feeling. Pushing myself to the door and knocking loud enough everyone in the house would hear it, the door opened and I fell in. From what Jenny and Duke told me, I got in just in time, too.

I heard Jenny talking, but I was breathing too heavily to hear what she was saying.

After I got my clothes back on and some water followed by a glass of Maker's Mark, Jenny's story began. She told everyone how she yelled at the cop for coming in her yard during that time of night. She told him to go away before she leaves the dog back out. That did the trick and he left. It was funny that she did not have a dog, but who cared at that point and time.

I was calm enough to tell my little adventure with every twist and turn. How I had to outrun the cop and all the little details I could think of. I thought it was an impressive story, but Carri only had one question. She asked if I finished the jumping jacks.

Everyone knew what it meant if I did. If I told the truth, other than being chased around Gibsonburg naked and cold, I would not get my reward. Instead, I would owe her a dinner at any place of her choosing. We made eye contact while I thought about it. I came to the conclusion that Carri did not seem to be putting on a bad girl act and I wanted to see if I was right. That is why my buddies groaned and the girls laughed as I said I only got to seven when the cops came.

It was getting late and everyone starting to feel tired. Duke and Jenny went to her room. Mark and Stacey went to a spare bedroom. That left Carri and me in the living room. She laid down on the couch and I sat in a reclining brown chair. As I was looking around for a blanket, Carri said "You know the couch is more comfortable, as long as you don't try to start anything."

It would be warmer with her on the couch and more relaxing. I just needed to make sure I didn't fall off while we slept. It would be a surprise if I didn't take her up on her offer. As I crawled under the blanket with her, we started to talk differently than we had before. Being just the two of us, there was less pressure to be a certain way and we could be more open.

Carri was talking as we laid together. "Jenny told Stacey and me about Sara. I am not looking for anything long term and I don't think you are either, but we can spend our time together and help each other deal. I am going through a loss too. My boyfriend died in a car crash at the end of summer." She sniffled a little and pulled my arms tighter against her. I liked what she was thinking. No more games dealing with other people and we could lean on each other. We both understood that at our age, everyone expects you to get over things quickly, but some pains don't just go away.

I simply said "Yeah, that would be good." She yawned and was asleep. I would have been out too, but my mind was running a mile a minute. I thought about Sara and how John would be coming in to meet up for business in about two weeks. Now I had someone who wanted us to be each other's emotional balance. Carri was what I needed at that time. We would have something over the other if either one of us went off telling people what we talked about.

It all ran through my head and a bunch of what–ifs played out. I must have fallen asleep at some point because I blinked and the sun was up. Jenny and Stacey were cleaning up while Mark was in the kitchen making something for breakfast. It seemed as though the excitement from my adventure the night before had pushed the alcohol out of everyone's system. At least enough that no one seemed to have a hangover.

Sliding my arm out from under Carri who was still sleeping, I got up and the girls smiled at me. It was if they thought they had found out a new secret that they were proud of. Once I was off the couch, I began to put my shoes on before walking into the kitchen.

Mark smiled at me and as he turned the bacon, asked for details. I guess I had a reputation that something would happen. Mark waved his hand to say come on. I picked up a piece of bacon and told him we talked then fell asleep. He seemed not to fully believe me, but he accepted it. After that, he pointed to a pile of pancakes.

He seemed happy as he was cooking. I felt bad that I needed to ruin his day. "Mark, I want to give you a heads up. You can't say anything to anyone." I took a bite of the pancakes and they tasted perfect. A little butter on top of them and nothing more needed. Enjoying the pancakes, Mark agreed to not say anything, so I told him.

"John out of New York knows Deatz is getting his supplies from someone else. It will not end well for anyone involved. I know this because John's delivery guy told me to call John. I told him everything and when he asked about you, I told him you were still with me. You only knew about Deatz going to Chicago to meet a new supplier.

Mark got a glum look on his face as I let it set in. I didn't wait too long as I wanted him to know everything before the girls came in. "Mark, I can sell you anything you want at my cost. You can still make money or you can go to the guy in Chicago, but I can't know about it till afterward. Either way, you will no longer have to worry about Deatz." I ate the rest of my food as Mark made more pancakes and bacon. I wanted to get more of the bacon, but I wanted to wait until Mark started talking. Not that I thought he would, but I did not want him to throw hot yummy bacon grease in my face. It might hurt and that was not something I wanted.

"Bearman, grab the bacon, I know you want to. I don't know if you caused this or if you got involved, but I need to figure out what to do. Don't worry, I am not going to say anything to Deatz. I want him gone too. He is an ass hole who made his own bed. How about you come over to my place tomorrow and we can talk more about it. I don't want to do it here. Can you let the girls know the food is ready? I want them to eat before Duke gets up, since he loves bacon more than you." Mark was not in a great mood, but he was also not angry. I could tell that in his voice. He sounded like someone trying to understand everything.

The girls did eat before Duke woke up and Carri was awakened by Stacey and Jenny. They wanted to get details like Mark and that is what kept them from coming in. Jenny got Duke after she ate while us guys cleaned up the kitchen. I decided to get on my way while everyone else hung out longer.

Carri wanted to get going too and I gave her a ride back to Fostoria. We might have only been a mile out of town on Route 300 when she asked what I told my buddies. To have some fun, I said that we had a wild night and it took everything we had to keep quiet. She looked at me amused as I finished with "I told them you did things to me that I would only dream about."

That got her to laugh and she told me that it must have been in my dreams because I was poking her in my sleep. Carri in a cocky way said that I must have said the same thing as her. "We were talking until we no longer could stay away." Now that got me to laugh. That sounded so much better than what I said.

The drive was fun in a way I had been missing. No matter how close you are to your friends, there is a completely different connection to a special girl. It is even more if you have a girl you're sexily attracted to. Most of our conversations were us giving each other a hard time. I had mentioned that I was going to go buy a truck after I dropped her off. She insisted on coming with me. She said that it was her job to make sure I did not buy something that was sky blue or anything girly. I was going to ask if I was the type to buy something girly, but she would have just made another smart-ass comment.

I pulled into Dodge dealer when we got into Fostoria and parked my car. We got to the first used Ram when a guy came over to us. He must have thought I was not serious about buying. When I asked what I could get if I paid in cash, he pointed me to a car that was selling for three thousand. He would let it go for two thousand for me just for that day only.

Since he did not ask how much I wanted to spend or what I was looking for, I walked away from him and into the dealership. The first person I met said he was the manager, so I asked him if all his sales guys are dismissive asses. That got his attention and he had me explain what I meant. He looked at me and asked how old I was.

I was raised to be polite until I am not being treated the same. So, I asked him if my age matter if I have twenty thousand in cash. That changed his tune and we went back out to look at the Rams and Dakotas. We walked for about thirty minutes when we came to a used Dakota with some custom work. It had been traded in about three days before. It was a pretty extended cab Dakota with a blue and silver paint job.

I was in love with it before I even saw the inside. Carri ran up to it so she could be the first to see inside. She opened up the door and climbed into the driver seat. She played while the manager and I walked around the truck. He seemed to keep being caught off guard with me. When I started talking price before we even started the truck, he kept saying how he would have to check what they paid for it. Finally, he got tired of me asking about how low he would go, he went to get the keys and look up the information on it.

The three of us took the truck for a drive. When we pulled back into the dealers' lot, he accepted eleven thousand out the door for the truck. We shook hands and he went in to do the paperwork. I went to my car and counted out the cash. My old car was not worth much more than five hundred dollars. When I was asked if I wanted to trade it in for two-fifty, I said no. There was a guy who I knew could use it more than I could use the two-fifty.

Carri seems to be having fun with everything. While she played and the manager started the paperwork, I called the guy I was thinking about. When I called the number, I had for him, his mom answered the phone. She got him for me and I asked if he wanted my car for nothing. All he had to do was fix it up. He was so happy and had his mom drive him over that very moment. The dealer's manager agreed to help with the paperwork to transfer my car to the other guy.

I never knew buying your first car could be so exciting. My first car was given to me and was meant to get me around till I saved up enough to buy a better car. It must have been exciting for Carri as well. Opening my new

to- me truck door, Carri grabbed my face and gave me a big kiss. Then said that "If anyone asks, I kissed you first because you took too long to kiss me." Yep, I was not expecting that and as I was thinking about it, she shut the door again.

Now with a smile, I walked back into the dealership with a smile on my face. The guy who first came up to me walked over and told me how sorry he was that he assumed I had no money. I told him how I no longer cared. When he started to walk away, I asked where the coffee was. I don't know if he really did feel guilty or upset that he lost a sale, but he offered to get me a cup.

We wrapped everything up at a reasonable time frame and got my buddy set up to take my old car. Now all I needed to do was drop Carri off and go home for a shower. I only hoped my mom and step-dad did not ask too many questions about the new to me truck.

CHAPTER TWELVE

THE TIME SEEMS TO BE going slowly while waiting for John to come. It had been a week since I told Mark about John coming and Deatz being dealt with. I got my mom and step–dad to accept that I got a loan from my boss to get a reliable car. Everything still was looking good for me.

Carri and I had spent a few evenings together talking and hanging out. The most sexual thing we did was kiss. We liked each other, but we still had memories holding us back. The story of how her last boyfriend died came up. That seemed hard for her to tell, but at the end of it, she smiled and hugged me. Since she had already told Stacey about her boyfriend's death, I didn't have to relive it with her. Plus, it didn't sound as rough to deal with as the whole thing she went through.

I went to Mark's house the following day as I agreed. We talked about everything on our minds and what we both planned to do. That was not a fun time for either of us.

Mark said he was going to get his supplies from the guy out of Chicago. When I asked why, he told me that he found out that Jay had been selling. Mark knew that Jay would try to screw me over. After Deatz is gone, he could tell Jay that Deatz was killed because he owed money and went against the wrong person. Mark was hoping that would scare him enough to straighten him out.

I accepted his decision, then I took him out to look at my

truck. Mark told me on our way out that he wanted to keep Jay on a path that he can watch him better.

Mark told me how he had become worried that his brother would get into something he won't be able to get out of. That only leaves him to do what he could to help his brother. I made two promises to Mark. The first promise I made him was that I would always be there to cover his back if he needed me. He thanked me for that. When I told him that I will supply him at my cost and even bring him back as my partner he seemed to like hearing that, but told me that he will not be considering those two promises.

As I left Mark's house, it felt strange. We had only been friends for a short time, but it felt as if I was walking away from a friend I knew my whole life. The things we did made a bond I thought was unbreakable. I also felt a concern when I turned on my truck. Looking at Mark's house one more time, I noticed Jay on the porch giving me an evil glare. The feeling I was getting from looking back at Jay was the same feeling I got when someone ran at me to fight.

When the week ended, Carri and I went to meet up with Duke and Jenny at a party in Fostoria. It was at a friend's house of Duke where the parents seemed to never be there. The guy who lived there had at least one party a month. Any given day people were stopping to smoke weed or drink and kickback. This would be the monthly party. From what Duke told me, it would be a big one.

When Carri and I got to the party, it must have been about eight at night. I could see people moving around and hear some Goo Goo Dolls playing as we walked up. When we got into the house, LL Cool J's Doin' it started. Everyone seemed to be having fun.

Carri saw someone she knew and took off. I stood there for a moment looking around when two of the guys I had covering different areas saw me and came over to me.

I didn't know they knew each other, but I found out that one of them called Mick to get some product. Mick did not have anything to spare, so he gave him the number to the other guys we had. That led to them setting up a meeting at the party. It was weird that they naturally did what I wanted them to do. They told me all about it and how they planned to reach out to the others. They wanted to set up a meeting so they all knew each other. That is when I promised I would take care of that and talked to them about us being a family. They liked how I wanted us to help each other out and protect one another. I added that I would be there for them any time they needed me.

That made them laugh and they told me how using my name seemed to help resolve a lot of issues. One of my guys said he starts every deal he does with "Bearman seems to be very involved with what I do." If someone doesn't know my name, they tell a few stories and rumors about me. The other guy agreed with him, so I took it as he was doing the same. My rampage over that month must have done more than I thought it did.

I secretly got excited that my plan had been working. I just imagined what I could do if I kept going on the same plan. As I said before, I could not believe how fast things happened in this business. Then out of the back of the house, I heard some screaming.

Walked back there to see what was happening. A girl had a knife against the throat of some skinny guy that looked so weak that a hammer might be too heavy for him. The girl was screaming and the guy kept saying sorry. I watched to see what she would do till she said "Do you know who my father is? My dad is the police chief of this town. I could cut you and nothing will happen to me. I should cut you so you think twice about grabbing my ass."

I figured since I still had my jacket on, if she tried to cut me, it would just damage my jacket. I walked over to her and squatted down above the guy's head. I looked at him and said, "You are just a dumb shit and I bet you realize that right now." The girl and guy both looked at me confused, but the girl looked more upset that I was getting involved.

She started to yell at me too about how I should mind my own business. I explained that she is affecting my business by making such a mess. She put her hand on the guy's throat and pointed the knife at me. I guess I will call them "my guys" who started walking towards the girl. They grabbed her and shook the knife out of her hand. It was a pocketknife with a lock blade and it landed next to the guy she was pushing the knife against a moment ago.

The guy on the ground went to grab the knife till I smacked him and told him to hold still. I could not help but to chuckle when the Police chief's daughter yelled: "YEAH YOU SHIT." She started to calm down so my guys let her go. I introduced myself and she seemed to have heard my name but could not remember why. As she kept asking why she knew my name, I asked my guys if they could give the guy a brief lesson on manners. They were happy to oblige, and picked him up to take him out back.

I told her not to worry about who I was. I said I was happy to stop her from facing attempted murder charges or assault with a deadly weapon. The girl was not too bright because she told me how her dad had got her out of trouble like that before. He kept trying to send her to something called Anger Management classes. We had been talking for a short time when my guys came back. They told her that he should have better manners now and they told me they would catch up later. She asked how she could thank me for explaining this to her dad.

Carri came up to me from behind and poked me in my side. I let the girls introduce themselves to each other. After they finished, the Police Chief's daughter asked if Carri was my girlfriend. Looking at Carri, I asked what she wanted to be called. Carri said, "We can go with saying I am your pretty and very special date." Then she kissed me, pointed over to the couch, and ran off again.

Before I walked off to see why she went to the couch, I said "You know, if you want to do me a favor, I would love to meet your dad. I always wanted to meet a Police Chief. That would be a great way to say thank you." I found a piece of paper and a pen on a tiny desk that was just off to the side of where we stood. I gave her my number and she left to go back to her friends.

I don't know if I was cocky, since I already had two cops on my payroll, and I was thinking the Fostoria Police Chief would be next. Thanks to his daughter being a mess, I would bet that he did some illegal things to protect her already. He most likely would not mind doing more shady work and get an additional payday at the same time. He might like to have a friend who is not burdened with the worries about the law. I would be more than happy to be that friend.

I would have thought more about getting the Police Chief on my payroll except everyone stopped me a short distance from where Carri was. With every few steps I got in, I could see Carri talking to Jenny. A few more steps and I saw Duke next to Jenny talking to two other guys. When I got in arms reach to one of the guys Duke was talking to, Duke came over to help me get to them. He wanted to introduce me to his new friends.

Away from the crowd and with my friends, Jenny stood up and gave me a hug. While she sat back down, I gave Carri a kiss and thanked her for stopping that crazy girl from hitting on me. She smiled and told me she liked seeing the look of disappointment on her face. I will never fully understand females, but that was fine with me. With a smile on my face, I turned around to meet the two guys.

My mood went from being relaxed and happy, to being defensive. One guy was taller than me standing at six foot four inches, brown hair only a few inches long. Duke said the skinny guy's name was Jon Rigg. He put out his hand and told me everyone calls him Riggs.

The other guy was glaring at me and started to show his teeth. Duke stopped introducing him to ask him what was wrong. I didn't give him time to answer by telling him how nice the scar on his face was looking. Duke was listening and blurted out "You are the guy that tried to rob Bearman? You said you got that scar from a group of guys that jumped you."

I could not help myself and laughed from Duke's expression while saying that and how Dan reacted. It was like all his anger had been replaced with embarrassment. Dan tried to explain his story as he stood there, and I loved it when he said it was two against one, which was Mark and me. He started to shrink until I stopped him. "Dan, it was just me that beat you up. My business partner at that time pulled me off of you in fear of what I would do to you. I am willing to let our past stay in the past if you are. Just keep in mind that I am more dangerous since we last met."

Dan reached out his hand towards me and told me he was sorry. I accepted his apology and took his hand. Duke and Riggs seem to relax, and started Joking about making bets on a fight between Dan and me. The rest of the party went on with no other major events. Carri told me she heard the rumor of me taking a brick shard to some guy's face. She told me she believed that it was a rumor that grew from just a small little fight.

I explained it happened when Sara disappeared and my anger had the better of me. She understood what I meant and how that happens. A nod from Carri and she squeezed my arm as if she remembered her rage after her boyfriend died. When I noticed that her smile and positive personality disappeared, I gave her a kiss on the cheek.

I told her "We are here, and no one is ever gone as long as you remember them. Remember the good times or the bad will consume you."

That seemed to help her and I gave her another kiss to remove a teardrop. She knew what I was doing and smiled at me. Carri went back to talking to Jenny and I moved toward the guys to talk.

Hopefully, Dan learned his lesson and he would not make me regret anything. Duke, Riggs, and Dan were laughing and it seemed as everyone was having a good time.

Other than a few bad glances from Dan, we got along and I knew that it would not be an easy path for us to be friends. That is if Duke kept in contact with them. I did not see me reaching out to Riggs or Dan. Riggs seemed like a good guy; I would not be trusting him considering who his friend was. I may forgive someone, but I don't forget and Dan was the person who got the worst of my rage. What I did to him was also something you don't forget.

The party ended around midnight like normal, but Duke, Jenny, Carri, and I left around eleven, which was when most people either started to leave or passed out on the floor. It was like most of the parties I had been to at that house. Duke and I tried to keep our drinking to a minimum. With the girls, we did not want to get drunk so we could get them home safely. Before we got on our way, we stood in the middle of the street saying our goodbyes. After a few hugs and the girls trading a few final details, we went in different directions.

Carri and I drove through Fostoria as she recapped the party, and what she and Jenny talked about. I sat there quietly glancing between her and the road. I caught myself thinking about how she was growing on me. I still loved Sara, but Carri made the pain a little less. I knew that we were only support for each other, but with everything going on, I forgot to be guarded against her. It did not help that she grabbed my hand from the center console of the truck and wrapped her hands around it.

We pulled into the parking spot in front of her place. We

got out of my truck so I could walk her to her door. I would not allow her to walk alone in her neighborhood at night. The thing she didn't know is that I had my .380 strapped to my ankle in a holster. I know most people would run if a gun was pointed at them. The others will stop if you put a bullet in their knee or shoulder. I remember being told that there is no such thing as a fair fight.

I got Carri to her door and she had the door open when she asked if I would come in to make sure the house is empty. I was a little confused, but I agreed and came inside. As we walked through the apartment in a tour or search, she told me how her mom had left. She said her mom went to her new boyfriend's house in another town. Carri was proud of her mom and I could easily tell that, as she told me about her mom earning her college degree. Then she told me about how her mom found a new job on the other side of Findlay.

As we finished going through her place and not finding anyone hiding, I stood in front of the door. I was waiting for her to come kiss me before I got on my way home. She instead told me she wanted me to double-check her room. I knew what she really wanted., I stopped her and told her that I was not wanting her to think I was in it for the long run.

She walked over to me and said she was not either. As she took my hand and led me to her room, she told me how she felt safe with me and how she did not want to be alone. Plus, she added how she wanted to feel some passion again. She set an alarm so I would get up and out before her mom got home.

Even though I had gone on a few dates since Sara had gone, I had not done anything more than giving a girl a kiss on the cheek. Carri said she wanted passion and our night was filled with it. I don't know if she thought the same thing, but it was as if we both were with someone else. As different as it felt to be with Carri, it had a small familiar feeling. We were happy afterward and felt comfortable with each other. After laying there talking, Carri fell asleep in my arms. I must have fallen asleep shortly after that. I was not ready to wake up, but the alarm went off and gave me no choice.

I looked out the window to see everything still covered in darkness. It was only six-thirty in the morning, so I don't know what I was expecting. I started to get dressed after pulling myself out of Carri's hold. When I sat back on the bed to put my holster and shoes back on, she woke up. All she said was that she didn't know I had a gun on me and she would call me later. I grabbed my shirt and jacket, and kissed her on the lips. Before I pulled away this time, I made her smile. I said "You better call, I would hate to feel used and thrown aside. I don't want people to think I am easy."

I didn't realize how cold it was at six-thirty in the morning as I climbed in my truck. The heater started to blow out cold air and gave me a shiver. I didn't want to sit around too long, and I shifted my truck in gear and got on my way home. It would be interesting to come up with a story to tell my mom what kept me out till the morning. If I got to my step-dad first, I could tell him I was with the girl I had been seeing. He might save me and handle explaining it to my mom or he could give me hell and I would have to deal with everything.

I don't know why I was hoping my parents were asleep. I knew well enough that they always got up early and gave me a hard time if I slept past nine in the morning. When I walked in, both of them sat at the table talking. I knew I had no good excuse and before I said anything, my step-dad Paul told me that Duke called me.

Since it was common that I would say I stayed with him or Mark, I figured Duke said something to Paul. When I started to say why I was out all night, Paul told me to get cleaned up first. I was not going to argue. What teenage guy wants to explain to their parents that he slept at a girl's house the night before? That would only lead to a bunch of awkward questions.

My mom never did ask me why I was out all night. Paul said he understood, then told me "Don't be stupid and be safe." With a nod, I went up to get some sleep. I did not get a lot, but a little before I was awakened to get up and help with fixing some things. I might have acted as if it bothered me, but I learned so much while helping to fix things.

CHAPTER THIRTEEN

ON SUNDAY, I TALKED with Carri about what happened between us. We agreed that everything was good with us and if either of us has too much of the past that catches up to us, we could be there for one another again. I told her it might be best not to wait till the past catches up to us again. We both laughed about it and made plans to go have dinner.

Normally I don't get too many phone calls, so, when I got a page from some number in Fostoria after hanging up with Carri, I had forgotten that I gave my number out to the crazy girl saying she was the Police Chiefs' daughter. She was reaching out to tell me how her dad wanted to meet and thank me for getting her out of a bad situation. That made me nervous and happy at the same time to hear. It meant I could make him the offer I thought about and get him on my payroll. It could also go the other way and end me up in jail.

I had just gotten out of the house and almost to my truck when I got a page from Mick. I drove up the road to a payphone to see what he needed. When Mick answered, he didn't waste any time and said he had a few guys calling him trying to get more product. It seemed as we had another growth in our business.

Mick ran down the list of what everyone was wanting. We discussed how much back stock we should start to hold onto. From listening to what Mick had been hearing, I decided I would make some changes. We would need to increase our deliveries from John to keep up.

It was about time that I would need to place an order anyways. I called and left a message for John. I requested the person on the other end of the line to let John know I needed more product and I gave the person the number to the payphone where I would be waiting. Luckily it was next to a little store where I could pick up a pack of cigarettes. I went in and was happy to see they had one of that instant cappuccino machines. It was new for this little store and made my day.

When I came back out, I heard the phone ringing. I don't think I was in the store for more than five minutes, so I was not expecting a call back so fast. When I answered the phone with a hello, I heard "Is this Scott Bearman?" Once I told him I was, a very gruff, impersonal voice told me to hold on.

I had enough time to light a cigarette when John came on the phone. He wanted to see if there were any changes and any issues he should be aware of before coming out. I told him that I was lucky and got a state patrol and a Fremont cop to work for me. He was happy to hear that. He got happier when I told him that I was going to have dinner with the Police Chief of Fostoria on Thursday. After explaining to him about the Police Chief's daughter, I gave details of what kind of trouble his daughter gets into. I told him of rumors of how he had to bend some laws to keep his daughter out of jail. John said he was impressed with me.

John also told me that he would be happy to have dinner with me on Thursday, too. Of course, I told him that I would be happy to have him with me while doing this. The truth was that having him come scared the crap out of me. I was not sure if he would be helping me, studying how I do things, or what. What could I say other than great?

Once we had that out of the way, I told John I would like to change my order amounts and schedule. The way we were growing, I wanted to do about twenty thousand an order and move it from two times a week to three. He had no problems with us doing this. He even made a few jokes and laughed at some comments I made.

By the time we finished talking, John told me that he would be coming to Ohio Wednesday night. First, he would go to Columbus, Ohio for some other business. Thursday he would be coming up to handle his Northwest Ohio business. I knew well enough he was talking about Deatz. He continued by telling me how he had to figure out who I would need to go through next. I was not too worried since I had built a relationship with John. This meant the next guy would not be able to push me around. However, It was not the time to ask about that. I would just have to wait and see.

He handed the phone back to the first guy I spoke with and gave my order to him. I don't know if he was being an ass or just trying to be smart when he told me that it was about time I got my orders up. He hung up on me before I had a chance to even say anything. I will go with him being an ass.

Since it was Sunday and I only had a few days left before John got here, I needed to make sure I had nothing going on Thursday. My first person to reach out to was Mick. I had lower margins with him working under me. I also knew how we were growing and whatever he took off my plate, I would be back to making what I had before. I also would not have the stress or time restraints to top it off.

Once I got a hold of Mick, we figured out where we could meet and discuss things. He told me he had to meet a guy named Kyle and after that, we could meet at the subway that was at Route six and twenty-three. The subway restaurant was included inside a gas station and a truck stop. I thought about it after I hung up with him. Why would he want to meet way out there if he was in Fremont? Then it dawned on me, Mick was covering all of our guys in the areas north of Bradner while I went south. That place sat in a great place for him to have our guys meet him. It was a well–

known location and easy to get to.

It did not take me long to get out there, so I decided to make some calls. My saving grace to avoid the payphone there was I knew the guy working at the subway counter. He likes to buy weed off of me sometimes and from what I have been told, he would sometimes buy product with a little more kick. The guy most likely would be working at Subway for most of his life. He was not too bad while doing drugs, but I could see him someday going overboard with it. It is not something people like to talk about, but people like him would keep looking for a bigger high till he was dead.

As I walked in, the guy I knew was behind the counter working with another guy. They were getting everything clean and killing some time. I figured I would be nice and gave them a joint so I could use the office phone. It never failed and they ran off. While I had use of the office, I got to set up a few meetings for later. I tried to reach out to Duke and Mark, but they both had plans to spend time with their girlfriends. That is how it goes, at least when you're young and dumb. Girls tended to fill most of our thoughts.

I used to joke with Sara that as a guy, I know we do stupid shit to impress a girl. She would laugh at me every time and asked if that was my excuse for doing stupid stuff all the time. I did not have the heart to tell her that a lot of my stupid acts were because of my crazy nature. I would tell her yes so I could see her smile.

After I stopped thinking about Sara and got my stuff around, I went out to wait for Mick and steal a cookie. I might have felt bad about taking the cookie or using the phone as I had until I saw they both were as high as a kite. I could have made a few sandwiches and they would have never cared. Instead, I only took a cookie and sat at a table to smoke while waiting for Mick.

He must have been rushing to meet me because I had just finished my cigarette when Mick walked in the door. He seemed to be excited when he sat down across the table from me. Mick covered all Fremont and had a group of guys that he worked with. What made him excited was that a buddy of his had agreed to help him take care of Fremont.

From what Mick told me since we had gotten two cops on our payroll, people trusted us more. It didn't hurt that I already had three people arrested when trying to move in on Mick's area. With those people gone, Mick had more demand to sell. That is why he said he had this Kyle guy come in. That is what made him so excited and I was glad that he was growing his area.

Once we got down to our schedule, Mick agreed to cover some of my guys to make sure they would get their deliveries. We made our agreements of the trade-off I would give him for covering me. Mick did not want much, but he did ask if he could meet John. I tried to be as nice as I could, but I told him that I would try, but he shouldn't hold his breath. He seemed to be let down from my comment.

I could not risk having anything go wrong on my side of things, at least not with John involved. I would not be asking John to do anything he didn't already plan on doing.

I still needed to figure out details with the police chief so he would agree to my offer. I also needed to get arrangements ready for the restaurant we would have dinner. Of course, the Police Chief wanted to have dinner at a steak house that was always busy and hard to get in.

Now with arrangements lined up with Mick, I could go wrap up everything else. Not that I was looking forward to it, but I had to meet my guy in Findlay. He was having an issue with some guy who owed seven hundred dollars. The guy refused to pay since he already used the drugs. I hoped that I could resolve this nicely, but I felt my luck was running thin.

The drive to Findlay was not too long of a drive, but it was long enough to think about a few areas of concern. One of the people that got in my head was Deatz. I had done some shitty treatment to others, but I had not killed anyone. I had not even seen a dead person unless you count TV. I could not think about how John or his guys would deal with Deatz. I figured they would kill Deatz and I did not want to be around for that.

I was about a mile out of Fostoria when I got a page. I had forgotten about having that pager, I jumped and hit the brakes of my truck. I would have been pissed, but when I looked at the number, I knew it was Deatz. I expected him to call me. I owed him two grand and I told him I would bring it around by the weekend.

I would have turned around and gone to his house, but I didn't want to see him and I had issues to take care of. It might sound bad, but I also did not want to give him money since he would be dead soon or at least I thought he would be. I felt that it would be a waste to give him that money since I could put it to better use. That is why I called him when I got into Findlay.

It is interesting how different people sound to you at different times. When I first met Deatz, his voice put fear in me. I thought he was the scariest person I knew. Now I knew that I had become scarier than Deatz. When I called him, he started yelling at me. I thought about using the same command he always had me use to make his dogs stop from attacking. That might have been a touch too much, but it would have been funny to me.

Instead, I listened to him. He said "You son of a bitch. You said I would have my money this weekend. The weekend is about over and I don't have my money. When will you be here with my two thousand dollars? Don't make me come looking for you."

Normally I would have told him I was on my way or I would try to calm him down. All he wanted was to have people fear him and kiss his ass. He was easy to fool too, but I had had enough of him. While he was on the other end of the line waiting for me to answer, I thought about what to say. Then I said it.

"Listen Deatz, I have something to take care of. If you want to come looking for me, I can tell you where I am. Just remember that I am no longer that scared guy you met back when. I have done some shit and I am about to go do some more shit. I know you have heard the rumors about what I have done. Think about that before you push me. You have people you sell to. I have people who I made into my family. They might not go as far as I go, but they will step up for me."

I took a deep breath and wanted to see if Deatz would say anything. All I heard was some angry heavy breathing. That told me what I needed to know. Deatz would not come after me, but he was angry. I knew angry people do things without thinking. So, before it went any further, I told him that I would bring the two grand and the money for the next delivery on Thursday. He grunted and I hung up the payphone.

My adrenaline was pumping and I felt as if I could do anything. I got back in my truck and drove to meet up with my guy. Driving down the road we called the strip, I saw who I was looking for. He had sandy blond hair and was a little bit smaller than I was. He did not look to be a threatening person. It took me a moment to get turned around, but when I did, I parked behind his car.

I felt crappy as I turned my truck off because I could not remember his name. As I grabbed my .380, I kept trying to recall what it was. Of course, he had to cut down my time to think of his name. When I got out of my truck by walking to me and yelling "Bearman" while holding his arms out for a hug. I hated hugging people I was not close to.

I did the best I could not to do a full hug by putting my hand out. It lead to one of those half hugs where only shoulders touch and ended with a odd handshake between the two of us. Since I was trying to make my guys consider me family, I knew I had to get past certain things.

After that, we got down to business. It turned out that the guy who owed him money was in one of the stores where we were parked. I realized it was set up that way, and I kept asking questions to find out all I could about the guy. What drugs did he take, what kind of personality did he have, and could he kick my ass. The last one was very important for me to know.

I went in and talked to a guy with a shaved head who ran a general store. I was hoping that it would have been a guy closer to my age, but this guy was about forty. My problem with this guy being that much older was how he would look at me. I did not expect an adult to look at a teenager too seriously. That meant he would not make it easy on me.

When I walked in, I looked around and saw that it was only the guy I wanted to talk with, and an employee. I turned the sign on his front door to closed and locked the door before walking back. He must have seen what I did and started to yell at me while walking towards me. I let him get close enough to me that he grabbed my jacket.

That was exactly what I hoped for, too. He thought he was in control till he felt my little .380 pushed into his stomach. He looked down and put his hands up. He tried to plead with me and told me to take whatever I wanted.

I told him I was happy to hear that. As I walked him past the crap he was selling, I suggested that he had his employee drop to the ground and stay face down. He took my suggestion and by the time we got to his register, his employee was face down. I told him that he owes me seven hundred and fifty plus a fee for me to come and personally collect it.

I could see in his eyes at that moment that he realized what was going on. I told him twelve hundred should be good, and he started to argue about the amount. He followed with apologizing for not giving my guy his money. The young employee started to asked what was going on. Being in a bad mood by having to deal with the guy owing me money, I told him his boss owed money for drugs and tried not to pay.

That poor boy started to cry and said that he did not want

to die because of his boss being a druggy. It was not nice of me, but I told him to pick better people to work for and this would not happen to him again. That must have pissed off the guy who owed the money. He made a fist and looked at me as though he was preparing to punch me.

Before things got out of hand, I said "Pay me the money you owe, give me the tape to your cameras, and I will be gone. I don't know why you thought you did not have to pay your debts, but now here we are."

The shaved headed guy started to slump and that is when I knew he had given in. He walked to the register and rung up a refund of twelve hundred dollars. I watched him count out the money and put it on the counter. As I picked up the money, he asked me who I was. I don't know why that made me happy. With a smile on my face, I told him that my name is Bearman and I watch over the area for someone much bigger. Once again, I was able to add to my reputation.

I felt on top of the world by getting this resolved without causing any physical harm and getting the job done quickly. We walked back for the security tape in silence. After it was all done and I was about to leave, I reminded him that he should plan to pay first from now on. He walked me to the door, but I think he wanted to make sure I was getting out.

I thought about the gangster movies I had watched and as he opened the door for me, I stopped in the doorway. Before walking all the way out I stopped. I said to him "You know if you had a protection plan, you would not have to worry about these kind of issues. I will have someone stop by later to talk to you about that." He sighed as I left his shop.

Oh, how things kept getting better. I came to collect and I realized a new opportunity for me to make more money. I thought about how to build on my idea and what I could do to get more people to pay for protection. A few ideas came to my mind when I got back to my guy, but this time I remembered his name. "Greg, good sir, I took care of your customer not paying and there might be a business opportunity for both of us. Let me get a cigarette from my truck and we can talk about it."

Greg and I talked about how he would talk with the guy I just dealt with. He would offer a protection plan. Then we pick one store a week and send some other guys in to cause problems. At the end of the week, you go in and offer them a protection plan. If they don't accept your offer, let me know and I have a friend that is a firebug.

Greg got excited about shaking down shop owners for money. I made it simple for him to start. After he gets the guy on board who I just spoke to, he needed to get two or three guys looking for a bit of cash or some drugs. These guys would go and cause some trouble, but not hurt anyone. They would simply go in a shop and knock over displays, make threats, and promise to be back as they leave.

I went through what I thought he should do and how much to charge for protection. None of this was hard to figure out, but Greg seemed to look at me like I was someone finding the cure for cancer. By the time I finished telling him everything, I had a bad feeling he would screw up and get arrested.

It didn't matter, he would be a good starter to try this idea out. Plus if he did get arrested, he was under eighteen and would not be charged with anything staying on his record. That was a nice thing about most of the guys working for me. It made it easier to tell my guys that turning on each other would cause them more issues. Greg reminded me that I told him that.

He said "I remember what you said and if this doesn't work, I am not going to say anything. You said we all can make lots of money and I believe you."

That was nice of him. We did another kind of hug like we did when I got there and I was back off to get other tasks done. It seemed to be a productive day. Now I only had to worry about Deatz. I figured that Deatz would not do anything till I came to him with the money for the next delivery.

I wondered as I drove back toward Fostoria, would John let Deatz know that he was coming? Then I started to play all the scenarios that could happen in my head. Living in the country among all the small towns could be nice and there was always time to think.

I started to worry that Deatz would come after me if he saw me when I was in Fostoria. Then it dawned on me that he had no idea what I was driving. Deatz had yet to see my new truck and most people did not even know that I got rid of my old car. Knowing that I could drive by him without him recognizing it was me made me relax, and I realized I could focus on my business and not him.

E.A. Maynard

CHAPTER FOURTEEN

IT WAS FINALLY THURSDAY. Between John coming into town and the meeting with the police chief in Fostoria, I was on the edge. I didn't think I would have done well in school, so I skipped it and got my day in order. I spent my morning working on making sure my list of who got what was ready for Mick.

Luckily, I did not have to rush and got to enjoy a nice breakfast at the Bob Evans in Fostoria. Since I knew a few of the girls there, I was not rushed out. They would also give me free drinks and sit to talk with me when time allowed. Relaxing early in the day helped. One redhead in there would sit and talk to me the most. She also got away with it more because her mom was the manager.

One thing I learned was that sometimes orders are messed up on purpose. If someone's order was wrong and got sent back, the staff could eat it. Most times the customers would notice it before eating it. That is why the only thing I paid for that morning was a twenty-dollar tip.

I would have liked to see Carri before doing anything else, but she was in school as was almost everyone I knew. To my surprise, when I walked out of Bob Evans, there was Deatz across the street in the Dairy Queen parking lot. It was easy to tell it was him as he sat in that pimped out old Cadillac. The car had over sized rims and custom green paint job. He even had something put in the paint to make the car have sparkles.

If I had to guess, it looked as he was getting ready to do a deal himself. It was funny to see if that was what he was doing because Deatz once told me how he was above street deals and that was what people like Mark and I were for.

I had heard that some of his guys had left him and were working with some of my guys. They paid more for the drugs, but I was told they felt more protected. Deatz might not have cared at first since he was still getting his money, but he obviously cared now.

I could be wrong and he was waiting for the Dairy Queen to open in a few months which made me sad. Not that Deatz was there but I had to wait till summer for a blizzard. Then again, I could always go to Wendy's and get a frosty with fries. Nothing like dipping your fries in a frosty.

Deatz didn't notice me staring at him and I decided to go before he did. Plus, the steak house I planned to take John to and meet with the Police chief had the staff coming in. That meant I could go in the back to talk with the owner. The owner of the steak house also ran the illegal casino, and I knew him well. He would call me if someone wanted something, but most times he had what he needed. I kept him well-stocked at a great price. In turn, he would send people my way.

When I walked in, the employees looked at me like I was crazy. The chef started walking towards me looking as if he was ready to kick me out the door. That was till one of the guys stopped him. I don't know what he said, but the chef turned around to go back to the kitchen.

I didn't have to wait long when the owner came in the door behind me. By the time I turned around, he already had his hand on my shoulder and was leading me to his office. While we walked, he said my name as if he wanted everyone to know who I was. "Bearman, you S-O-B, you being here means you finally need something from me!" He finished saying that when we entered his office.

We sat down in a rather plain office. Boxes lined the walls between two file cabinets and his desk. It was night and day in comparison to the office he kept for his main business. I guessed that he needed to keep up more appearances when dealing with people who were gambling and getting a rush. In the restaurant, you just needed to show that money is coming in. His restaurant made good money, too. It seemed to never have an empty seat. I never was able to get in, but I did not speak to the owner either.

This time, I talked to him personally. I needed to make sure I got in and everything was taken care of. When I asked him for the favor, I also promised to return the favor. His smile told me that he already knew what favor he would ask. After about ten minutes, we got everything out in the open. I think even our bond to each other had strengthened. I had learned that the Police Chief would be fine with taking money and looking the other way. There was a reason the illegal casino never had issues with the police.

When I walked out of the steak house, I had two dinner reservations. One was for the evening and a table-side greeting from my friend. I also agreed to take John to the Illegal casino. The other was for Carri and me. I wanted to take advantage of getting a table while I could.

The rest of the day left me with time to kill for at least for the next five hours. My dinner with the Police Chief and John was at six o'clock. I decided to go and clear my mind at Mosier Lake. Plus, I was in the mood to relive some memories.

While I was there, I must have dozed off. I was awakened by my pager going off. It was only three, but I felt as if I had slept for much longer. Maybe the stress of everything had knocked me out. Either way, I got myself straightened out and drove to the hotel down the road where they had a payphone I could use. As luck would have it, when I got there, the payphone was out of order. The front counter clerk agreed to let me use the hotel phone, but it cost me ten dollars and a joint.

Listening to the phone ring, I wondered who it was. My guys put a code at the end of the number to let me know it was them. This number looked like it was from Carey, Ohio. When I called, the voice was of a guy whose voice I had heard before. It was the same guy who answered the phone last time I talked to John. He was as charming as last time. It didn't matter because John got on the phone before we had a chance to say another word.

"Bearman, I am in some little town called Carey, I think. I will be in Fostoria soon. I want you to meet me at Deatz's house. I want you there for everything. You need to see it; I want you to remember." I didn't respond or even make a noise, and John hung up when he finished talking. The guy behind the counter of the hotel just looked at me as I put the phone on the receiver.

I didn't want to be there to see whatever John would do. I could not imagine that it would be pleasant in any way. There was only twenty minutes left until it was time to meet at Deatz's place after the call. I was only five minutes away, so I left the hotel and went to get a gas station cappuccino. The day had become gloomier than I thought it was earlier. It could also just have been in my head, but it looked as if there might be a storm coming. I don't know why I got so focused on the weather. Seeing the clouds rolling in and blocking out the sun had me feeling a little down. It might sound morbid, but I thought how much better it would be to die on a sunny day.

Thinking about my body covered by the rain and the cold air running over my body, made me feel as though I was just another piece of trash left out. Whereas on a sunny day, having your body laid out taking in the sunbeams, may be sad, but it's like God is embracing you. That is why I guess I also started to feel bad for Deatz.

This stuck in my head for the few blocks that it took me to get to Deatz's after I got my hot cappuccino. When I pulled in, Deatz sat on his porch. He was wearing a shirt that looked like the opening scene to Saved by the Bell. His jeans looked like any other pair, but he wore a belt buckle that looked to be a gold crown. It appears that he was trying to say that he was the big boss, the king of the business. That is when my feeling bad for him went away.

As I got out of my truck, he yelled at me asking about my truck. I was sure that he would be ready to fight or kill me after how I spoke to him. I started to wonder if I was the only one still bringing in money. Mark had left and started doing his own thing and was using the guy from Chicago for his supplies. A good portion of his guys had moved to work under me for the protection. He might have had a few people still running for him, but I was the only one still making anything, at least compared to him and anyone he had left.

Walking up to his porch, I thought about the first time I walked up and felt scared. Now I felt pity and justification. Deatz still wanted to throw his weight around, so he asked with a rough tone what I was doing at his house so early. He did not look happy when I told him that the guy delivering had requested to meet at his house. That scared him and I could see it in his eyes and facial expression.

Deatz began to ask what I was told and what I knew.

His questioning stopped when a black Cadillac Deville pulled up. It looked as if it just came out of the factory. Two guys got out of the front of the car and a heavy-set guy got out of the back. I assumed the guy getting out of the back had to be John. Deatz jumped up from his seat and walked past me, so it was not a far leap to take. John had to be just over six-foot-tall and close to two hundred and thirty pounds. He walked as if he was in his own neighborhood. I guessed that John had been in the military since he wore his hair in a military cut and is what I had been told is called a high and tight.

I walked to John as well and when I reached him, I put my hand out. He took it. I was not sure if he meant to squeeze it so hard, but if he put any more strength into his handshake, I would have had broken bones. Once I told him who I was, he smiled and leaned in. In a quiet voice, he said that he looked forward to talking after everything was done. I was not going to show it, but I took a breath of relief. I would not have to worry about him killing me. We walked together into Deatz's house.

Watching them walk in with Deatz first and John behind him, it was easy to see Deatz had given all his control over. I would have sworn John was in control of everyone once we all were in the house. He seemed to be used to being the one that took control. The guys that came with John covered the exits of the living room without a word. John sat in the recliner as he told Deatz to sit on the couch. Me, I stood between the TV and the window across from the couch

Deatz was in the middle of everyone. He would look back and forth between John and me as if he was trying to figure out what was going on. I don't know how long we stayed silent, but it felt like hours. I flinched when John started to talk. He said "Do you know why I had to come here? What error you made to force me to come to see you?" Deatz talked about his sales going down and tried to blame it on me. Then he started to mumble that he knows he had not grown the business as he promised he would.

John stopped him. "Detrick, you know why I am here. Your sales didn't drop, but your orders did. You betrayed me and the trust I gave you. I know you went to someone in Chicago. Did you think I would not notice anything? Did you think that I would let this betrayal go without doing anything? Or did you just not think? That must be it, you didn't think."

I know I should have been focused on every detail John was saying, but I just found out Deatz's real name is Detrick. I wanted to make a joke, but looking around the room, there would be no laughing at this time. Plus, I lost my thought about Deatz's real name when I heard rain hit the window behind me. Thankfully the sound of rain cleared my head because John got up and walked over to me.

John put his hand on my shoulder and told me that it was time to show him who I was loyal to. It was made very clear to me that I had to hit Deatz and keep going till I was told to stop. I thought about how my hand would start to hurt before Deatz would feel much. I had to figure out what to do and I looked around the room. Then it dawned on me. I picked up a county phone book that laid next to the couch. The yellow cover and thin sheets inside were made big enough that I had to use both hands to swing it and have any effect.

I gripped that phone book as hard as I could and swung it like a bat. I swung that book from above my shoulder and down till it hit Deatz in the face. I didn't realize how much force it must have had because Deatz flew off the couch and onto the floor from the first hit.

The two guys helped Deatz up to the couch and I repeated the process. By the fourth hit, blood was running from his nose. After a few more swipes across Deatz's face, I had to stop and rub my shoulder. I went to switch the direction and as I was about to swing the phone book down again John stopped me before I took another swing. I was glad he did, too. I had not done so much damage to someone before without being filled with rage. Deatz looked horrible. Blood was coming from his mouth and his nose, then his eye on the right side started to swell up. As bad as he looked, his anger was easy to see and it was focused on me.

As I stepped away, John sat next to Deatz and asked him what he promised when they started working together. Whatever that promise was, it could not have been good. Deatz dropped his head and I heard him start to whimper. Seeing a man as big as Deatz whimpering made me feel uneasy. He took everything I gave him without a tear. All I got from him was a grunt here and there. John's words had more power than all the pain I could cause him. That might also be what made me feel uneasy.

Nothing more was said between the two. John got up and lead me out the door. His two guys stayed inside; I didn't want to think about what was going on or what would happen to Deatz. When we stood next to John's car, he told me to open his trunk and unlock my truck. He wanted to get out of the rain. As he climbed into my truck, he said that we have work to do. I did what he said and as I was grabbing the duffel bags out of his trunk, it dawned on me that he said "We". It also dawned on me that I was getting drenched.

When I got in my truck, I pushed the duffels in the back seat and started my truck. I really hoped that the heat would not take too long to get going. I was going to start to drive, but before I did, I had to ask. "John, forgive me, but what did you mean that we have work to do? What I do is boring with lots of driving between towns."

John was upfront about why he wanted to spend the day with me. He had plans for the area. Some of it only involved me showing a presence so it was clear John had someone watching his interest. With that answer, I took off down the road and out of Fostoria. It only took me about ten minutes after I got out of town until I reached a barn that sat between two fields. The farmer used it to store supplies and a few pieces of equipment. Since it was not farming season, no one would be around.

Pulling up to the barn, John gave me a funny look as if I was crazy. I knew the farmer and he had given me the code to get in. When I got it opened, I pulled in and turned on an electric lantern. I started getting everything broken down and repackaged for my guys. While I worked to finish the task, John walked around with a flashlight. He was fascinated by everything he saw. I would have sworn that he never saw any farm equipment before or had ever been on a farm.

I had gotten good at breaking things down and could do it in around forty-five minutes. I joked that it took a pharmacy several hours the get me a prescription, but I could have a few grand worth of drugs separated and ready to go in half an hour.

We would have been back on the road to meet with Mick, but John wanted to discuss different types of farming equipment, which went on for twenty minutes. Then like a flipped switch he walked to my truck without another word. I closed the barn door and we were on the road again.

I explained to John what I planned for the day. He kept asking about our meeting with the Fostoria Police Chief. We discussed what I had heard about the Chief's daughter and how the illegal casino had been paying off the Chief. There were no details that I left out since I know I would want all the information I could gather before going into any event.

We talked about several topics on the drive. Come to find out, John was a hockey fan and had season tickets to the Rangers. I will admit I was impressed. I had never been to a professional sporting event. John also had two kids and a wife. The picture he showed me was of a beautiful family. His wife looked as if he picked her out of a modeling catalog. The kids looked respectful and were lucky to get their looks from their mother.

When we got to Fremont to meet with Mick, the rain had stopped. Mick was running late, but that was nothing new. To add to it, Mick thought I would be coming on my own. While we waited, John took a puff from a cigar and told me something I never knew. He said "Scott, do you know why I care about doing business in this area? As a boy, I got sent here in the summers for a month to stay with my aunt. She lived in Fostoria on Fremont Street. We drive around town to go to her friend's houses and as we did, she always pointed out this one old house. Oh, it was a beautiful house, too. She would tell me that local legend said the house was built for Al Capone's mistress. He would come and stay in Fostoria and even started an underground casino."

I was impressed and had more respect for Fostoria. It felt odd that John was being this open to me after he just had me beat the crap out of Deatz and most likely had his guys kill him after we left. Mick finally pulled up next to my truck.

At first, Mick was being his normal self and making jokes with me. That was till John got out and walked around. I got a look from both of them. I had a bad habit of not introducing people. This

139

was one of those times, but Mick jumped in and acted like he just met some big celebrity. It took a few moments to get Mick to calm down and act normal. Once he did, I unloaded what I needed him to deliver for me and what he needed for his guys. I got the money Mick owed me and we all left.

It was getting close to my reservation time with the Police Chief. When we got out of Fremont, John started to tell me how dinner would go and what my part would be. The plan would be to make an offer of five hundred dollars a week and some bonuses for a few favors. That is exactly what John offered him, too.

To my surprise, John and the Chief got along like they were old friends. The owner of the steak house even joined us. I was hoping to blackmail the Police Chief, but John made an alliance where we all came out ahead. When we finished, the Police Chief told John and me that he is a friend of the Chief in Fremont. He said his friend might want to have the same deal. John gave him a smile and said, "I think we can do the same for your friend."

When dinner was over, I drove John back to Deatz's house where his two guys were waiting. John got out of my truck and looked me square in the eyes. He told me how people like Deatz should not drive after drinking and I thought that was an odd comment, considering he was not the type to drink. As I sat there not sure what to say, he got into his Cadillac and drove off. The day was about over but a new phase of my baseness had just begun.

I stopped to get gas on my way home and went in to get a pack of smokes too. I knew the guy behind the counter and he told me that just an hour ago, a car went off the road and caught on fire. The firefighter who came in told the clerk that the driver had to have been drinking. He talked about how there were vodka bottles everywhere. That is when I knew what happened to Deatz. I also knew that I would have to accept and deal with the fact that I had a part in his death.

CHAPTER FIFTEEN

I HEARD SOME PEOPLE talk about Deatz's car accident. They said it was something more than an accident, but most people accepted the story. It was not long that no one even thought about him.

I grew my business by getting everything direct from the source now. I had also started a counterfeit operation after John had helped me buy a property and set up everything. Duke took over the printing. I would work with him to put out counterfeit money when he got behind, but Duke was the main guy in that area.

We no longer were a bunch of kids pushing drugs, we were a small crime family. We even had our connection to a real mob family, but only Mick, Duke, and I knew about that. People seemed to like to think they know who was at the top of the ladder.

Things with Carri went well till her mom got a marriage proposal from the guy she had been seeing. Carri and her mom left Fostoria quickly after that. I would like to say that Carri and I kept in touch, but that was not the case. The day Carri moved out of Fostoria, we gave each other a kiss and without another word being said, I left. We never saw each other again. We filled each other's needs and we both knew it. We had helped each other get past what held us back.

As for Mark and me, we had stopped talking and hanging out. He had made a deal with the guy from Chicago. This put us at odds with each other. Mark did not mean to create a small drug organization, but he did and he became my competitor. I gave everyone working with me only one rule when it came to Mark's group. No one is to touch Mark, but anyone else is fair game. This made things rough between us, but we managed to stay out of each other's way most times.

With the strength and loyalty of my guys, no one challenged us. I believed people knew I would have done anything to make sure nothing would take it away. Other than needing to rough some people up now and again, things had become smooth sailing. The only problem I was having was with my real family. Everything I was doing in my private life had taken its toll.

It is on to the next adventure and all the secrets that come with them.

FINAL AUTHOR MESSAGE

Every story has a begging and mine was in the small town of Risingsun Ohio. I go into more details about my history at www.eamaynard.com if you want to learn more.

I have been telling stories ever since I was a young child. It was not till I was an adult that I felt like writing down a story. Once I did, I had written Country Secrets (eamaynard.com/book/country-secrets-3/}. It gave me so much to complete, I found writing a prequel gave me the same joy.

I will be working on putting out more of the Bearman series for you the reader to enjoy. There are two things I hope you do if you enjoyed this book. The first is go buy Country Secrets and keep reading. The second thing is to give a review for this book. Other people decide to read books based on what you have to say. Plus, I want to read it too.

Finally, thank you and I hope to keep entertaining you with my stories.

Bearman Series:

- **Bearman**: A Road of No Return
- **Country Secrets**
- **Aftermath**: The Stories After the Story

www.ingramcontent.com/pod-product-compliance
Lightning Source LLC
Chambersburg PA
CBHW052009240626
47153CB00008B/2810